INDEFINITE

NIGHTS

Patricia Ferguson was born in Virginia, USA, but grew up in England. She trained as a nurse and midwife, and now lives in Bristol with her husband and two sons.

Her first novel *Family Myths and Legends* won the David Higham award, the Somerset Maugham award, and the Betty Trask prize, and her latest novel, *It So Happens*, was long-listed for the Orange Prize in 2005.

Other books by Patricia Ferguson:

Family Myths and Legends
Write To Me
Four Part Harmony
It So Happens

INDEFINITE NIGHTS
and other stories

Patricia Ferguson

Published by Back To Front
www.back-to-front.com

This edition published by Back to Front, 2006

First published by Andre Deutsch Ltd, 1987

The story 'Indefinite Nights' first appeared in *Fiction Magazine*

CONTENTS

Indefinite Nights 7

Patrick 29

The Products of Conception 45

The Quality of Mercy 57

The Dry Familiar Plains 79

Sister Hilary 95

Inside Knowledge 119

INDEFINITE
NIGHTS

'HERE,' he whispered. 'I was dreaming about you.'

'Oh yes?' I said.

'Yeah, we were on an escalator, we were going down and the walls were going up, these sort of great big granite blocks.'

'Which side was it last time, this one?'

'Mm, just a sec.'

'Okay. Here it comes. Waggle your toes.'

'Mr Haldane was there too, with one of those spotty dogs, you know, a dalmatian, he was carrying it, it was looking at me over his shoulder.'

'Is this sore?'

'No. It's okay. How many more nights you got to do?'

'Four, this stint.'

'Bump night tonight then.'

'Yes, all downhill after tonight.'

'Your name's Christine, isn't it?'

'Christina. Are you warm enough like that?'

'Yeah. Who's on this morning, is it Pam's lot?'

'Why, they your favourite?'

'Oh no, you're my favourite.'

'Ah, you say that to all the girls.'

'You bet I do.'

We smiled at one another, as if we had suddenly agreed about something. I suppose in a way we had. I remember I felt quite cheerful as I locked up the drug trolley, but then I often did at dawn.

Sometimes if it was quiet I'd open up the big glass doors in bay two and step out onto the balcony for a few minutes, just to breathe in some morning air. Once I stood there just before it began to rain, and thought that the air had a fresh tint of green to it. I saw a pigeon that day too, from above. I remember its pretty, muted back feathers, its clopping wings and small still head, all in flight through the clear greenish air, so far below me that for an instant I could pretend that I was flying too.

I went back into bay two but the telephone rang before I could get the first set of bolts undone. I checked my watch: 5.30. She was early.

'Rebecca Ward, Staff Nurse.'

'Ah, hallo dear, this is Mrs Brownlow, you know, Johnny's
mother – '

'Hallo, yes, he's had a really good night, I've just been talking to
him, he's fine.'

'Oh good, oh, thank you dear, is it Susan?'

'Chris.'

'Oh, hallo, Chris, I'm sorry to have disturbed you dear, I know
how busy you are – '

'No, that's all right. Really.'

'Well, I'll be in later, all right dear?'

'Of course, all right, bye now.'

'Bye-bye dear.'

I hung up and sat for a moment with my hand on the receiver.
We were really quiet that morning. I had two good students, Sally
and Jan, and an auxiliary, a surly sort who'd kept her name to
herself but worked well enough. West Indian, she was. She was
lumbering around now with the urinal trolley and twanging up
the blinds. Sally was doing the six o'clock signs and turning off
the dim red night-lights, and Jan was doing the teas. The
infusions were all on time. No one was dying. The CVP lines were
all patent. So I had a few unaccustomed minutes to myself, to sit
about sighing.

'Was that her again?'

It was Sally, leaning against the desk. She looked a bit wild, her
mascara all smudged in black rings round her eyes and her hair
falling down.

'Yes.'

Sally lowered her voice. 'Does she know?'

'Of course.'

She glanced back at Johnny's side of the bay.

'But he doesn't?'

'Bet he does. Bet he's guessed.'

'Why? What'd he say?' She glinted.

'Nothing. I just think he knows, that's all. You finished all the
signs, then?'

'Nearly. Give us a chance. Has the Gestapo been?'

'Not yet. Push off. I'm busy.'

'Jawohl,' said Sally, clicking her heels. She swung round and
goosestepped jerkily away into bay two and presently I heard her
giggling by Mr Dooley's bed.

I found the kardex under a pile of computer printouts and checked through my report. I was on indefinite nights, eight nights on, six nights off, and sometimes I felt I might forget my own name. But I knew all my patients well enough. Twenty-seven patients in all. Three single rooms, two bays, and the far end.

In the far end and the singles lay the least ill men. By day they limped about in dressing-gowns, read *Tidbits*, volunteered to give out the teas, took naps, idled. By night they snored, or wanted cups of tea, or aspirins. In the bays, nearer the nurses' desk to be under my qualified eye, lay the grots and sickies. The grots, the incontinent geriatrics, lay strapped into their beds in bay one, cotsides up, waiting to pop off. The sickies lay in bay two. That was where the real action was, as Sally would say.

Bed 10, Harold Fletcher, 54, for Mr Haldane, colonic re-anastomosis, fourth day post-op.; and

Bed 11, Brian Dooley, 63, for Mr Harrison, oesophageal varices (watch out, could blow at any minute); and

Bed 12, Joseph Miller, 72, for Mr Haldane, carcinomatosis, not for resus., does not know; and

Bed 13, John Brownlow, 22, for Mr Haldane, carcinomatosis, on cytotoxics, not for resus., does not know; and

Bed 14, empty tonight and

Bed 15, Henry Goldbloom, 58, for Mr Haldane, query carcinoma query stomach.

I shut the kardex up and checked the time again. Only 5.40. I thought about a cigarette. There was still Mr Colonic Washout to be seen to, down in the far end, but he was all Sally's this morning, I'd only have to oversee. I ferreted around under the desk for my handbag, and the double doors at the end of the corridor bashed open. She always opened them like that, smacking at them with her two broad raised palms.

'Achtung,' murmured Sally, passing me.

Footsteps clumped.

'Good morning, Sister.'

She rolled up, nodded.

'Staff.' She was a nasty sort, that Night Sister, a happy blackleg during the last NUPE strike, manning the dinner trolleys with a glad Dunkirk-spirit smile. She picked up my report and slouched sourly round the ward without speaking.

'Untidy ward, nurse,' she said to me, back at the desk. 'Locker tops. Do something about it.'

'Right, Sister. Good morning.'

'See you tonight.' She stumped off. I went to find Sally in the sluice. She had the trolley all set.

'Talk to him all the time, okay? He's embarrassed to death and scared as well, he natters all the time. So talk back, all right?'

'Right.'

'And hold the out-end against the side of the bucket so's it makes less noise, see, no splashing noises.'

'Right.'

'You're all right?'

'Look, just go and have your smoke, okay?'

'You mind your manners,' I said, and went.

That day while I slept Mr Colonic Washout had his gastrectomy and came back from theatre more dead than alive, and was put into bay two next to Johnny; and Mr Dooley, 63, for Mr Harrison, burst his oesophageal varices during a ward round ('Went off with a real bang,' said the Late Staff at report) and shot fountains of blood over half-a-dozen terrified medical students and, as it happened, Mr Harrison himself.

'All over his Savile Row,' added the Late Staff reminiscently. There was a fleck of dried blood over one of her eyebrows, I noticed.

'Bed 12, Mr Miller, you know him don't you, he had a good day ...'

Johnny had had a good day too. Two of the day students, when they'd washed their arms and faces and turned their aprons inside out, had sat on his bed and explained what oesophageal varices were, and how Johnny personally was not to worry about them, or about Mr Dooley or in fact about anything at all, ever.

So Johnny told me anyway.

'Hallo, Chrissy.'

'How you doing?'

'Wonderful. It's all go round here. A real show.'

He talked about Mr Dooley for a while.

'Blood always looks worse than it is,' I said. 'It always sort of spreads around and looks like pints and pints – '

'It *was* pints and pints.'

'I'm sorry. I wish you hadn't seen it.'

'He's going to be all right though.'

'He's doing really well.' I touched Johnny's hand. There was another beaded bruise on his forearm where one of the infusions had slid through the vein and pushed 5% dextrose into his flesh. Both his slender arms were covered in bruises and scars, as if he were a junkie. Which of course, at the time, he was.

'I due a shot?'

'Not yet. An hour's time.'

'Good-oh. See you then.'

I checked his infusions, timed them. They were running well. He had four of them, two in each arm, and a nasogastric tube strapped to his cheek, so that anything inside him could come straight out without causing him too much trouble. Fluid drained from it, slowly, constantly, a pale brackish liquid with a mysterious admix of dark flecks.

'Mint sauce,' said Johnny, seeing me eyeing it. I pulled a face at him and passed on to Mr Colonic Washout, newly incarnated now as Mr Geoffrey Chester, 57, for Mr Haldane, Ca stomach and complete gastrectomy, knows.

'Hallo.'

'Hallo, nurse.'

'Got any pain?'

'No. I'm fine, thank you.'

He lay there afraid to move. Only his eyes moved. He had a tube down too, connected to a suction machine beside the bed. I bent down to look at it. It was a small machine, with rather a fetching action, clean little wheels busily revolving.

'All hooked up,' said Mr Chester, his eyes straining down at me. I straightened up.

'It's sort of to give your insides a rest. To keep you all empty inside, to give the stitches a chance. Are you thirsty?'

'Bit.'

I gave him a quick mouthwash.

'Put your tongue out, right out, that's right — '

I gently swabbed his cracked old tongue with glycerine and lemon. He kept on staring up at me, and I saw that the pale grey irises of his eyes were ringed with cream. Arcus senilis, I thought, that's interesting, I must remember to tell Sally and

Jan to have a look ...

'You're an angel, you are,' said Mr Chester suddenly, as I cleared the swabs away. I gave him a little smile and shook my head, but still I felt my insides all relax with pleasure. I felt smooth all over. Well, who wouldn't? It had been an impulse of love that had made him speak.

Touch the sick tenderly and they will be grateful; not grudgingly, as if you had lent them something or done them a kindness, but purely, physically grateful, with a gratitude indistinguishable from love. A limited and temporary love, of course, but vehement, perceptible even when undeclared. It doesn't happen all the time. But it happens often enough. It's love-without-strings, the basis, perhaps, of all our calling: love-without-strings, the nurses' perk.

'Right now. Ring the bell if you need anything. If you get any pain. You let me know. All right?'

'Thank you, nurse. Thank you.'

'Anything at all. Just ring the bell.'

Love-without-strings.

No time for such tender scenes the following night. Night six, that was. A night to remember.

Report was twenty minutes late.

'Sorry about this,' said the Late Staff. She had been crying. 'It's like World War Three in there,' she said, gesturing over the desk at the bays. There had been a death. One of the grots lay limp and yellow behind his curtains.

'He was gasping all afternoon,' said the Late Staff, knuckling at the mascara under her eyes. 'He's only just gone, we haven't had a chance to do him. Oh, and Jan Geeson called, she's not coming in, she's off sick.'

'Oh Christ,' I said.

'I tried to get you someone else, but no joy yet.'

'Aux?'

'Irma.'

'Oh bloody hell.'

'I know. Sat down the far end with the *Daily Mirror*. I'm sorry. Look, I'll just get on with it, try Night Sister, you've got to get someone.'

I began to tremble. Report was twenty minutes late, even with three student nurses, two staff nurses, and the aux; I was being left with the aux, and Sally. And it was drug night.

'It's bloody drug night,' I said out loud, interrupting.

The Late Staff shook her head, and went on. I wondered if I was going to cry too. There were infusions running in two of the single rooms, and three blood drips – that meant observations every fifteen minutes – in bay two, where Mr Chester was brewing a cardiac arrest and bedsores and everyone else had multiple infusions or CVP lines. Two colonic washouts and an enema in the far end, and five incontinent grots and a stiff; and it was bloody drug night.

'So good luck, that's all I can say,' ended the Late Staff. 'See you in the morning.'

'If I last so long,' I said.

I sent Sally to check the far end and went to run round bay two, where two of the infusions had already stopped and Johnny was 500 mls behind on one of his, the yellow one with the vitamins in it, but that was Day's fault, not mine.

'Hallo, Chrissy.'

'Hallo, can't stop tonight, sorry,' and I whipped the bandages off Mr Chester's forearm and stroked his blocked vein until oh thank you Lord the spasm relaxed and the drips started again but no such luck with Mr Goldbloom's stalled juices next door, and now everyone on blood was due signs again, and it took me four minutes, fast as I was, and that meant four minutes taken out of every fifteen until the bloods were through and two of them ran all night and the other didn't end till 4 am.

Sally came in.

'Far end?'

'Quiet mostly. Coupla drugs at midnight.'

'Single room's calling. Check the drips too.'

'Right.' She tore off.

I felt a great lifting wave of affection for her and ran with it into bay one thinking that if I could just get through the first hour everything would be all right, but then I saw the drawn curtains and remembered again that it was drug night: I must go all through the drug cupboard, the stock cupboards, and the refrigerator, opening all the little bottles and packets, counting everything, pills, ampoules, powders, bandages, elastoplasts, rubber gloves, and re-order the shortfalls in triplicate, or all the following week nurses would be running out of essentials, and cursing, and chasing all over the hospital to forage; and someone like Johnny would be kept waiting for pain relief, for attention, for comfort.

I held on to someone's bed-table and said to myself, Now, don't panic, don't panic. Keep calm, call Night Sister, beg and plead, get someone. Call Night Sister, call Dr Whatsit for Mr Goldbloom's drip. Don't panic, don't panic.

I ran back to the telephone – don't believe all that old stuff about nurses never running, I'd have used roller skates if I could've got away with it, in fact on busy nights I often fantasized about it, shooting down to the far end with an enema bag and my trusty wheels – and called Dr Whatsit, who said she'd come round when she could but probably not for an hour, by which time, I knew, Mr Goldbloom's drip would be hopelessly out of kilter but Baldy Haldy'd just have to lump it, and then I tried Night Sister.

'You called me.'

'Yes, oh Sister, I'm so short-staffed, I've got so many ill patients and we've had a death, please Sister, I need someone.'

There was a pause. I could hear her breathing.

'Well,' she said at last, 'there's no one to send. I'm sure you can cope.'

'Sister, I can't Sister, please.'

'Look, I'm sorry, it's impossible.' She sounded huffy already.

'Well then Sister, can I leave the drugs out, could I do them tomorrow?'

'Of course you can't. Out of the question.'

'But it's dangerous, we can't see to them all, there's only me and a student – '

'Nonsense. We can't all have perfect staffing levels, nurse. Just do your best, I'm sure you can do that. You've got an aux, haven't you?'

'Yes, but – '

'Or I can report that you are unable to efficiently manage your ward.'

Silence. My heart's going to burst.

'Nurse?'

'I'll do what I can, Sister.'

'I'll be along presently. Do buck yourself up, nurse.'

Buck up, I mouthed at the receiver as I crashed it down. Buck up, fuck off!

And I'd wasted time. I ran back to bay two, where someone was wailing: Mr Goldbloom had wet the bed and was close to tears. So was I. I ran and called Sally and charged back with the linen trolley and we changed the bed in record time but we were out of clean pyjamas so Sally had to pound down a floor to male ortho so that Mr Goldbloom's shame could be covered.

'I'm so sorry, nurse.'

'Please. Don't worry about it.'

'You're so busy.'

'It's not your fault.'

He went on apologizing and glooming until I could've slapped him and said, For God's sake shut up and go to sleep! And then there were drugs to give out. I ran around with the trolley, Oh, why not roller skates, I could arabesque along the corridors, my arms stretched out in front, the tray with two red-and-black bombers and a mouthful of water held out before me like a crown on a cushion.

Old buffer down the far end: 'I can't get these pink things down, lovey, they're that big.'

'Take some more water then, Mr Bulford.'

The next lot of blood signs were due two minutes ago. I motion Sally to go and do them, which means I can't give any more drugs out until she gets back to check them. My hands are shaking. Old buffer tilts his head back, waggles his cheeks from side to side.

'Gone?'

'No, dear, sorry.'

'Never mind, just take your time,' I say between clenched teeth. 'That's all right.'

It was about then that I realized I could manage everything, just about and skimpily, if I didn't take any breaks and cut Sally's down to fifteen minutes, just time for her to throw her egg-and-chips down and maybe buy me a sandwich to eat while I did the drugs. I began to feel a bit better and even managed a smile, I remember, when the old buffer forced his last horse-pill down.

'That's the ticket, Mr Bulford, sleep tight!'

That was night six. I was running on air by dawn, high as a kite on not eating and coping against the odds: drugs as potent as any. Sally and I got the giggles over the early teas and sang 'Morning Has Broken Like the First Morning' in quavery soprano voices as we shot up the blinds, and when Mr Fletcher opened his gummy eyes and said, 'Where's me morning kiss?' Sally pranced over and gave him one.

Of course the drips were all hopelessly out and one of the colonic washouts had been more of an enema really – 'Just relax, Mr Pointer!' for Christ's sake – but the drugs were all done and everyone was more or less clean and dry and if some of the urine bags were close to bursting well all that bloody troop of day staff could cope. So I told Sally anyway.

I remember I felt like hugging her goodbye when we finally got off duty, and I know she felt the same way about me. You see it often enough in war films, that simple comrades-in-arms love between soldiers who've shared a close look at chaos. That was how Sally and I felt, and if we never worked together again we'd still greet one another with real affection in twenty years' time, should we meet.

Perhaps it's the love that old soldiers meet to commemorate, rather than the battle? But old nurses don't have reunions. Though Sally and I could: not the Waterloo Dinner but the Rebecca Night Six Banquet, with food served in kidney dishes on mouth-care sets, and the champagne flowing like blood-drips.

That was night six.

Night seven wasn't much fun either, though things were quite a bit calmer. After report I went straight to bay two to check the drips and say hallo, but Baldy Haldy was there before me, glaring at the fluid charts at the end of Mr Miller's bed. Mr Chester, I saw, was on a waterbed, a very squashy affair. He lifted a feeble hand to wave at me and the movement bounced him gently up and down like a little boat at sea. He held his hand up, palm towards me, and bounced, his face grave.

'Mr Haldane.'

'Just what have you all been up to, these charts are ridiculous. I don't know why you bother to keep them, why we bother to write them, look at this!'

I looked. 1000 mls behind schedule.

'I'm sorry, Doctor. We were short-staffed.' It sounded more

like an excuse than a fact. 'I'm sorry,' I said again.

Baldy snorted, slammed the chart shut, dropped it on the bed-table and stalked off. I picked it up and hung it up properly and ran after him.

'Please Doctor!' I caught up with him in the corridor. He was a big man, waxy and pale-eyed.

'Well?'

'Oh, ah, Mr Chester. That waterbed.'

'*If* you nurses turned him every two hours as they did in the old days, *nurse*, he wouldn't need a waterbed!'

'I meant, it's just that it's so squashy, is he for resus.?'

'Of course he's for resus.'

'I mean, if he arrests, we can't do him on that bed, we'd have to lift him out —'

'Look, what's the matter with you lot, it saves you work, doesn't it, you turn him less, the CVP lines don't come to bits, what's the problem, nurse?'

I should've kept quiet. I should have realized I'd hardly have been the first to point all this out to him. But I went on: 'If he arrests, we'd have to lift him onto the floor, I don't know if —'

'Look!' Mr Haldane hissed. 'What d'you want, eh? It's my decision, is that what you want? My decision, he stays in the waterbed, all right?'

'Right.'

'Good. Goodnight. Nurse.'

And off he stomped. Well, I'd had a bad day too. I'd been too high to sleep for a long time. When I'd finally slept I'd dreamt about Johnny, that I was standing by his bed trying to get one of his infusions, the yellow one with the vitamins, to run on time. I was counting the drips and timing them as I so often did in reality, one . . . two . . . three, watching each arc of gold become the bead, each bead become, slowly, the heavy tear-shaped drop. One . . . two . . . three . . . and Johnny lying shadowy and slender in his bed, so close beside me I could've reached out and laid my hand upon his breast.

The dream had woken me up, and I hadn't slept again after it. Three hours sleep that day. My eyes were sticky, my legs ached.

'Achtung,' said Sally, passing me with the linen trolley. The corridor doors bashed open.

'Nurse.'

'Sister.'

She slouched around as usual. At the desk she said, 'That waterbed. Won't do. Too squashy.'

'Really, Sister?'

'I'll mention it to Mr Haldane.'

'Oh. Thank you, Sister.'

'Night.'

I gave her my nicest smile. 'Goodnight, Sister.'

Jan was back and the aux was good, so I spent most of the night in bay two, sweating over Mr Chester. His bed was surrounded by get-well cards. One of them was hand-drawn, a child's picture of Mr Chester in bed, a matchstick man all wired up, with his CVP lines, drains, drips, whirring pump, and catheter bag. Bandy triangular nurses stood about the bed holding trays, and GET WELL GRANDAD was written in tilted multi-coloured capitals across the top.

'We're losing him,' said Dr Whatsit, sighing by the desk.

'I'm scared stiff,' I told her. 'We pull him off the bed – if we can – and all his wires'll cross. It'll be a hell of a mess.'

She nodded. 'I know. Still. Maybe it won't happen.'

We looked at one another and knew that it would. A question of time, that was all.

He kept going, though, all that night. I washed his face a lot. He was nearly unconscious most of the time. Someone's grandad, sweating with death.

Johnny had a paperback. He was pretty lively, they'd upped his dosage, and he was still awake at one o'clock. I went over to him. He smiled at me. There was a little gap, I noticed, between his two front teeth.

'Listen to this, Chrissy.'

It was a poetry book. I recognized the cover, we'd used it at school. I wondered what fool had given it to him.

> 'Every Morn and every Night
> Some are Born to sweet delight.
> Some are Born to sweet delight,
> Some are Born to Endless Night.'

I looked at him anxiously, but he was grinning.

'That's you,' he said.

'What?'

'Says here.' He turned back to the book, frowned, appeared to read.

> 'Some are Born to sweet delights,
> Some are on Indefinite Nights.'

I laughed outright.

'You idiot!'

Johnny laughed too. 'Not bad for one o'clock in the morning.' In the light from the bedside lamp I saw how jaundiced his eyes had grown, how bronze his skin.

'You should be asleep.'

'I can sleep any time.' He turned to put the book away and I saw that his hair was beginning to fall out. There was a big pale bald patch at the back of his head. The pillow was littered with dark, shed hairs.

'D'you ever read poetry, Chris?'

'Can't understand it.'

'Oh, you don't have to understand it, I don't always understand it, I just –'

'Nurse, oh nurse!' It was Mr Goldbloom, poor leaky Mr Goldbloom.

'Oh, nurse, I'm so sorry, oh dear, oh dear –'

In the canteen that night a nurse I'd never seen before sat down beside me and said, 'You on Rebecca?'

'Yes.'

'How's Johnny Brownlow?'

I gave her a look. She had a fair fat face, with triangles of brilliant blusher on her cheekbones, and her hat was pinned low on her forehead in a saucy Edwardian tilt, sure sign, in that hospital, that she was a bit of a tart.

'Not so good,' I said.

'I can hardly believe he's still alive,' says this tarty sort, screwing her eyes up against her cigarette smoke. She wore lots of crumbly blue mascara. 'I was there,' she went on, 'when he come in. Appendix, they thought. Opened him up, had a look, and bam it's last rites and telling his mum he won't last the night. How long you been there?'

'About five weeks,' I said.

'So what they doing for him?' This was a new voice, someone across the table. I knew her vaguely, we'd both done a stint as students on the same ophthalmic ward.

'You've never worked on Rebecca,' I said to her.

'No, but everyone knows Johnny.' There was a murmuring round the whole table as she spoke, and I looked up and saw that, for once, everyone there was in on the same conversation.

'He's just so lovely,' said the student on my left. I knew her, she was a friend of Sally's. I looked at her, at her silly smile, and pushed away my plate.

'It's such a crying shame,' said the tarty one. 'I mean, he's so *nice* as well, he got to know my name, I never told him, he just got to know it somehow. I used to talk to him a fair bit.' She sighed.

'Does his girlfriend still come in?' Another new voice: staff nurse on Pettit ward.

'I don't know,' I said, 'I've only done nights.' I found my cigarettes. I was trembling a little.

'Every day she'd come in. Ever so pretty. A model.'

'No, she was an art student,' said the tarty one.

'It's just so sad,' sighed Sally's friend.

'What they doing for him anyway?'

'Cytotoxics,' I said. 'Then some sort of new-fangled radiation, I don't understand what, you know they don't tell you much on nights.'

'How's he taking it?'

'Jaundiced. His hair's coming out.'

'Oh no . . .' more murmurs, commiseration.

'Why don't they let him go?'

'They never know when to give in.'

'It's such a shame.'

I stood up, swung my bag onto my shoulder.

'Got to get back early,' I said, stubbing out my cigarette. The table was littered, dirty plates, cellophane, spilt water, flecks of ash.

'Tell him I was asking after him,' said the tarty one. 'Tell him Janet, bet he'll remember.'

I didn't go straight back to work, instead I locked myself in the staff toilet to try to think. I could not at first name the emotion that had made me tremble so in the canteen. It seemed to have too many strands to have just the one name, and I was not sure how far I really wanted to investigate them. I lit another cigarette: think.

I had been angry. Because they had talked about him, because I had joined in. We had tossed his name to and fro across that soiled table as if tragedy made him public property. We had used luxurious sentimental voices, the voices we might use to discuss any ersatz celluloid tear-jerker.

I had been surprised, too, simply surprised that he was remembered so vividly by nurses who hardly knew him, or who had nursed him months before.

Anger, surprise; I didn't mind admitting to them.

I balanced my cigarette on the china toilet-paper holder and stood up. There was a square of mirror over the sink and I looked into it at my scrawny white face and red-rimmed eyes. Third strand: jealousy.

Jealous professionally, jealous privately. Jealous, because his life was my responsibility, not theirs. Mine. My carelessness could kill him, not theirs. It was me that soothed him, not them. He was mine to talk about, not theirs.

And privately. Tell him Janet, bet he remembers –

I picked my cigarette up again.

And why, *why* did they all know him? The reply to that one was the most uncomfortable of all. Because he was young, and beautiful, and dying, he fulfilled all our most romantic notions of what nursing might mean. Only wartime fills hospital beds with beautiful damaged young men, and there was no war. Johnny was all we had: a lovely young man, unattainable, weaker than a child. Not just love-without-strings: romantic love-without-strings. Passion-without-strings.

There's something wrong about bloody nursing, I thought, throwing my cigarette stub into the toilet bowl. Or about nurses? Or about me?

I pinned my hat on very straight on the top of my head, and went back to work.

Night eight followed. My last night. My last night, as it happened, on Rebecca. I was moved the following week to a pediatric ward. No explanation was given. I didn't expect one. The Night Sister gave me a fulsome report; that didn't surprise me either.

The last night on Rebecca was the quietest I ever had there.

While I'd slept Mr Chester had arrested. It was 3.30 pm, they told us at report: visiting time. There were visitors everywhere. Mr Chester had three.

He was still on the waterbed. They tried to pull him up and over the bed-sides and he weighed so much it was like a tug-of-war with a corpse as rope; his latest blood transfusion unhooked and swung round, spraying Mr Goldbloom, who screamed, and the CVP line fell apart and tangled up one of the student nurses as she heaved at Mr Chester from one side, and tripped her so that she fell forwards onto him in the waterbed, and they couldn't hold him once they'd lifted him, but dropped him heavily onto the floor with a crash of falling drip-stands and bedside waterjugs and mouth-care trays ...

He died anyway. They had the fire brigade up – the cardiac arrest team I mean – running round in circles and braying orders and shooting drugs into all parts and (so it always seems) all comers. But he died anyway.

That was at 3.30 pm.

I came on at ten and Lord the place was quiet. As if the fright of Mr Chester's going had put everyone on their best behaviour. Or that, the Reaper having struck so wildly elsewhere, everyone else felt immune, if not exactly in good spirits.

So, come 4 am, Sally, Jan, and I sat at the desk with a pot of tea. The aux had her own tray down in the far end. It was the first time we'd managed this illicit treat all week. We talked about night six and Jan groaned and apologized. We ate buttered toast. It was so quiet. The far end slumbered, snoring in tune. The singles slept. The grots were all out cold. The sickies dripped in good time.

'It's the last night,' said Sally. 'We're leaving it nice for them.'

'Hush!' I said, but too late. Almost as I spoke there was a crash and a ripple of spattering noises from bay two.

'No, I'll go,' I said. I got up and went into the bay. At first all I could hear there was breathing. Mr Chester's waterbed had gone, replaced by an ordinary empty bed. His cards and flowers were all gone too. No one spoke to me. I crept about in the dim red light, checking. Not Mr Goldbloom, for a wonder. Not Mr Dooley, shrunken alcoholic Mr Dooley, paying for past whiskies with his own present blood. Not Mr Miller, no trouble, Mr Miller. Not Mr Fletcher, lonely Mr Fletcher.

Johnny was crying. I drew the curtain partly round him and turned the bright day-lamp against the wall so that it would give just a little light, and switched it on. He held one yellow skeletal hand over his eyes. He hardly looked human. Monday was barber-day, and Johnny had had his head shaved. It had given me quite a shock when I first came on duty. I sat down on the bed.

'Hey, hari krishna.'

He smiled at that. 'Hari hari,' he said back. 'Don't you like it?'

'I'm not sure,' I said.

'The barber came. It was all falling out, I reckoned it'd look better all off, see.'

'I'll get used to it. What did you drop?' The bed was soaked on the other side.

He gave a sob at that, and eventually said, 'Orange juice.'

'They're never letting you drink?'

'Just the taste,' he said. His yellow eyes filled again. 'I'm all sticky.'

'You're a daftie,' I said. 'I'll get some water. Just a sec.'

I went and filled a bowl, giving Sally and Jan a dismissive little wave as I passed the desk. 'Nothing serious.'

'You're lucky being next to the window,' I said to Johnny, as I cleared the locker top and put the bowl down. I'd change the bed afterwards, with Sally. I covered him up with the fleecy bath-blanket and slid the wet sheet off him from beneath it.

'Not really. I mean, I asked. I was over by the door, I asked to be moved so that I could see out.'

I took his flannel, wetted it, squeezed it out, gave it to him. 'Face,' I said.

'I can see the stars sometimes,' said Johnny, his voice muffled as he scrubbed away weakly at his eyes. 'Just before dawn, when the city's lights are, you know, lower. Mostly they're too bright though.' He passed the flannel back to me and I gave him the towel.

He dried himself and said, 'I wonder how far away you can see London. Miles into space, I reckon. Or those American cities.

Las Vegas. New York. I bet you can see New York from the moon.'

I soaped the flannel and picked up his left hand and washed it for him, carefully so as not to disturb the new drip in the back of it.

'I saw Orion once, out of the window. The stars, you know, Orion.'

'I know him,' I said. Johnny's palm was sticky with orange juice. 'He looks like Elvis Presley.'

Johnny laughed. 'What you mean?'

'The way he's standing there. Hips all slanted.'

'That's his sword-belt.'

'Nah, it's Elvis the Pelvis. A real star, see. Up there with all the rest.' I rinsed his hand, dried it.

'Like a neon sign,' said Johnny dreamily. 'A neon sign, like in Las Vegas. Orion in Las Vegas.'

I picked up his other hand.

'Ow.'

'Sorry. Nasty bruise.'

'Yeah, they were practising.'

'Well, they've got to learn somehow, you know.'

'You're rotten to me, you are.'

I started on his arms: long and very slender, like those of a slim girl, with long tender muscles just defined beneath the skin.

'Look at my needle tracks.'

'That one must've hurt.'

'It did. Here, Chrissy.'

'What?' I patted his arms with the towel.

'That Mr Chester.'

'Yes.' I tried not to sound guarded.

'I was thinking. My turn next.'

'Who says so?' I was smooth: you'd never have guessed how my heart turned over with fright.

'I say so.'

I folded the bath-blanket back and soaped the flannel again. I did everything slowly and carefully, trying to stay calm. If he asked me outright, what should I say?

'Why's that?' I asked. I began to wash his chest. There was no hair there, because of the cytotoxics; or perhaps he was just too young anyway. His skin was a deep clear bronze. He could've been a bronze image lying there, or an alien creature from another world, with his golden eyes and smooth skull and graven yellow arms. An alien creature. Only his weakness showed that he was human.

'I just know,' he said. I dried him and spread powder on his chest, as silky as a child's under my hand. I remembered my dream. I stopped where I was, my hand on his breast, my palm over the little dark nipple.

'They're going to irradiate me,' said Johnny lightly. 'I'm gonna glow in the dark.'

He grinned, and I took my hand away, and the crisis, if it had been a crisis, was over. I didn't really understand what had happened. I wasn't even sure that anything had.

I didn't think about it too hard either. There were no conclusions I wanted to reach.

I could've ended this story here: left it as an account of what a certain job was like. For me, I mean. I'm not claiming to speak for anyone else.

But there's a coda.

It happened six months afterwards: a Saturday in high summer. I'd left the hospital in the April, and hadn't taken another permanent job yet. I was doing agency work to keep going. I was really low that day. My boyfriend had just thrown me over. He was a medical student, in fact he was one of those sprayed with Mr Dooley's life-blood all those months before. We didn't talk about Rebecca though. We didn't talk about anything very much. Perhaps that's why we didn't last so long.

Anyway, it was a bright Saturday in July and I was at the library, too low to look smart. My hair had needed washing two days before, as well. Lord, I was depressed.

I was wandering up and down looking along the shelves and swinging my empty plastic bag when I saw a skinny God-squad type freak over by reference. I felt a bit scornful, all those shaven heads and rattling money boxes turn me right off. Then, as I got closer, I saw who it was.

For a moment I felt dizzy with sheer surprise. It was Johnny, of course. Jeans and a T-shirt. Thin as before, but upright, walking, no drips, no drains, no needle tracks. Johnny, his head still shaved, one skinny wrist out, leaning against the books, reading.

I felt no pleasure that I can remember, just shock. I backed quickly behind the thrillers and peered out, my heart pounding. He turned a page, intent. For six months I had hardly thought of him. I watched him, remembering: You can see New York from the moon. Orion in Las Vegas. Some are born to Sweet Delights, some are on Indefinite Nights.

I could've walked up to him, spoken his name: 'Johnny, for God's sake! This is wonderful!'

I remembered my last night on Rebecca, the lascivious tenderness of the blanket bath.

If I spoke to him, what would he say, what would he do? I had no doubt he would remember me. He would remember my name.

What would he say, what would he do?

He would look down at me, and smile, and judge me. He would notice me. I would no longer be extended womanhood, beyond judgement if not beyond love. He was a man again, able, if he so wanted, to ask of me everything I knew I would never give him, not him, not anyone. Indefinite Nights, that's me.

I honestly can't say whether I'd have behaved differently if I'd been happier or better-dressed. As it was I didn't hesitate. My heart was beating very fast. I backed some more, very quietly, and hid behind the great wall of engineering textbooks at the back of the hall, and stayed there until I was quite sure that he had gone.

PATRICK

WHEN I was a student nurse I worked for a while in a psychiatric ward. Something went wrong with me there, something failed me. The nurses' protection failed me.

Once, my flatmate, working on a renal unit, became so concerned about her urinary output that she put herself on a fluid balance chart. She told me about it, giggling. I laughed too. I was on a gynae ward at the time, and nearly every night stood naked in front of the mirror examining my breasts for cancerous asymmetries. We laughed over this as well, when I told her about it. Our concern was jokey because we had the nurses' protection: youth, authority, uniform, and the strength that passes from patient to nurse.

General nursing means that you're daily shown the messy power of body over spirit. But physical ills, by and large, can be treated. You can take away physical pain, change the wet bed, distribute sleep and comfort.

Also the physically sick tend to say sorry, or thank you. If they splash you with vomit, or helplessly soil the bed, they'll make some attempt – unless they're really almost dead – to be apologetic, or grateful, as you clear up the mess. Sometimes it's just a flicker of the eyes: sorry. They're signalling, really, that they've still some grace left, are still human, and acknowledging at the same time that the nurse too is human and thus subject to fear or disgust; an acknowledgement which makes it possible for us to pretend, somehow, that we are not.

Of course there remains some natural empathy. Sometimes you look at the patient and see yourself lying there, on the wrong side of the hospital sheets. But it's all essentially fraudulent. My flatmate examined her urine, and I my breasts, but we laughed about it. Because, while everyone believes themselves to be immortal, nurses believe it more. We have god-like powers over pain and fear, and are constantly shown that sickness is something other people get. And we all wear uniforms to underline who's where: patient in pyjamas, in bed; we in starched aprons, on our feet, immune, inviolable: protected.

Visit any hospital canteen at lunchtime and you'll see the protection at work. Straight from the cancer ward, straight from dressing the amputated leg-stumps of thirty-a-day men, a nurse will sit fresh-faced over a cup of tea, lighting up her Silk Cut or her Rothmans Kingsize, discussing death and sickness with tender detachment, with fraudulent empathy; with her nurses' protective immunity like a warm cloak round her shoulders.

When I was on Hardwick ward, the psychiatric ward, I lost my magic cloak, and had no protection at all. I avoid thinking about it now if I can. But sometimes I'm reminded anyway. I was reminded a couple of days ago, in fact. One moment I was sitting in the circle at the theatre, eating a lemon ice-cream, the next I was back on Hardwick, sitting beside Mhairi.

Mhairi lay on her bed most of the day, too drugged and mad to walk. She nearly always wore the same clothes, a brown polyester skirt, a yellow T-shirt, an acrylic cardigan with chipped brassy buttons dangling on their strings: jumble-sale clothes. Mhairi was very quiet, because whenever she spoke live rats hauled themselves out of her mouth, wriggled free with her every word. She saw them, she felt them. They were real rats, to her. So she lay very quiet, not asleep, just still, gathering energy for a fresh suicide attempt.

Mhairi favoured a violent end, but luck was against her. She had laid herself down with her head in the gas oven, and struck a match; and lived on, her face glazed and set with scars. She had escaped from the ward one evening, dashed down the main road in her dressing-gown and dived beneath an incoming tube; and broken her wrist.

Working on Hardwick ward meant keeping an eye on Mhairi, making sure that she was quiet and not getting close to another try. It meant making Mhairi stay alive so that the rats could go on crawling out of her. After a week or so on Hardwick ward I could hardly sleep at night for the rats I forced into Mhairi's mouth. And I could almost taste them myself. No cloak: real empathy.

There were other problem patients, on Hardwick. There was senile Henry, who ate orange peel and cigarette ends, but would perhaps have been happy enough if only we'd left him in peace. But we never would, because as well as emptying the ashtrays into his mouth Henry liked to crap himself. He did it all the time. And then we couldn't allow him to go stinking out the dayroom, putting the other patients off their lunch, we had to catch him and wash him and change him. But Henry ran off, fought back, clung to his trousers, stood barefoot in his loaded underpants, wouldn't climb into the bath. We forced him to be clean. We held him down and scrubbed him. We were forcing him to be human, and perhaps there's only so much humanity to go round; because in making Henry more human we became less so ourselves. That's how I felt anyway.

The hours were all alike on Hardwick. Most of the patients, variously depressed, psychotic, schizophrenic, hysterical, or addicted, sat all day long in the dayroom, dispersed on the sweaty plastic armchairs, waiting for time to pass, quivering with drug-induced Parkinsonism, shouting, laughing, muttering. We staff sat there too, desultorily chatting to the patients who weren't too mad to answer. Any stranger entering, it struck me more than once, would've had trouble telling staff from patients, since no one wore any distinguishing uniform.

Only when something happened, when a patient finally screamed and clawed at the air, or went for someone else, did it become clear which of the two sides we all were on. But such incidents occurred only once or twice a shift. For the rest of the time, unless it was ECT day or the doctor's visit day, we all just sat, mostly, waiting and smoking. Everyone smoked, all the time. The air was always grey and shifting, the carpet was pocked all over with burns. There was often a smell of scorching.

The doctor in charge of Hardwick ward prescribed ECT and drugs for his patients. There was no therapy on Hardwick ward, no basketry or finger-painting or role play or group dynamics or any of that stuff.

'I can't really see it doing any good either,' said Jenny one endless afternoon in the dayroom, 'but at least it would give us something to do as well.'

Jenny was another student. She had lost her cloak too. Once we had both spent a morning making Henry stay clean. We had forced him into the bath twice. He had soiled himself again, with an audible effort, half an hour before we were due to go off duty – Jenny had heard him do it. She had run and told me about it and we had gone off and hidden in the kitchen until it was time to go home.

'I just couldn't face it again,' Jenny had said. Jenny wore thick glasses that magnified her clear blue eyes. I didn't look into them because I had known what she'd meant: that the next time Henry maddeningly struggled, she might, perhaps, be unable to prevent herself from hitting him. I knew because I felt the same way myself.

'Honestly, I wish I could wear an apron,' said Jenny now. 'Doing Henry, I want a proper apron on.'

'R.D. Laing wouldn't like it,' I said.

'Sod R.D.Laing,' said Jenny.

Once I saw the Charge Nurse kick someone. An ex-patient came running up the path one day and halted outside the lobby, shouting and jumping up and down with directionless rage. It was a cold day, but he wore only a pair of greyish underpants. His skin was pallid, his head shorn. He turned up his face and mouthed at the sky, struggling with his arms as if he were drowning.

The Charge Nurse, a dark, sad-eyed Pole, went out to him. The ex-patient raised his fists and screamed, and the Charge Nurse knocked him over with one easy hand. While the ex-patient lay on the tarmac, face-down and shouting at the ground, the Charge Nurse quickly kicked him twice in the ribs, hard. I saw him do it. I was standing by the window. I saw him. I turned round to exclaim in horror at whoever was standing behind me, and there was no one there. It would be his word against mine, I realized almost immediately. Besides, who could I report him to? And who was I to report him anyway, when I was making Mhairi stay alive, and having so hard at poor old Henry with a scrubbing brush, and had already slapped him, in my heart?

It seemed to me then that I wasn't a real nurse any more, because I was no longer powerful or immune. I couldn't relieve my patients' pain, and I couldn't endure witnessing it. All I could do was share it. I felt I had to make up my mind which side I was on, that I could stay on the patients' side, suffer real empathy and go mad myself; or get like the Charge Nurse, a detached or brutal jailer. A choice for nurses only, I thought; not doctors, doctors can always clear off: it's nurses in the front line.

It was a bit like one of those nasty childhood word games,

> Which would you rather,
> Eat a snot sandwich,
> Or drink cold sick?

Which would you rather,
Be Elsa Koch or Mhairi?
Turn Nazi, or spew rats?

It was a measure, I think now, of how mad I had already become, that I never realized then how easily I could do both. So I saw the Charge Nurse kick the patient, and was outraged. But there was no one behind me, to corroborate me. I shrugged my shoulders, and was cravenly glad.

One day I was sitting with the little Bengali woman who had the bed opposite Mhairi's when Jenny called me. I had worked out earlier that if I went and sat with the little Bengali woman, and tried to talk to her, I would stop feeling so sick whenever she came near me. The little Bengali woman had cut off the end of her tongue with a pair of scissors, and for the first few days after her admission all she would do when approached was open her mouth very wide, showing the wet black stitches.

'How could she have done it?' I'd asked Jenny then.

Jenny had shaken her head: 'I don't know. I mean, it just keeps sliding out of your fingers.'

I'd nodded, and we had shared a shocked giggle; because I'd tried too, left hand as pincers, right standing in for the scissors. Jenny was quite right: cutting out your own tongue is a seriously tricky business.

Anyway I was sitting by the Bengali lady's bed, feeling sick but trying to look friendly when Jenny called me.

'There's an admission.'

'Need a hand?'

'If you like.'

I liked. I got up and smiled goodbye at the Bengali lady, who quickly looked away.

In the corridor Henry was standing, arms dangling, knees slightly bent, outside the sluice. The sluice door was locked because Henry wanted to get in there to retrieve the shitty trousers he'd been forced out of earlier.

'Hallo, Henry.'

'I want my clothes,' said Henry. He'd been saying so all morning.

'Shut up, Henry,' said Jenny, without rancour, as we passed.

'I want my clothes,' said Henry, as we turned the corner.

The new admission was slung between two policemen in the lobby. The policemen held him rather gingerly, at arm's length. They were nice-looking policemen, with red cheeks and nice thick moustaches. I wanted them to stay, I wanted to go on looking at them so that I wouldn't have to look at whatever it was that they held between them.

'This,' said the left-hand policemen, 'is Patrick McDee. Say hallo, Patrick.'

The new admission raised his head, just a little way. He wore a woolly greenish hat. His eyes were swollen almost closed, and his face was the scarlet lion-face of last-ditch end-stage alcoholism.

'He's not feeling too well, isn't Patrick,' said the right-hand policeman.

'And a little bit itchy,' said the other, gently shaking his charge by the shoulder.

'He's an old friend,' said the Charge Nurse, the sad-eyed kicking Pole, appearing very suddenly from the office. I tried not to look at him.

'I want my clothes,' said Henry catching up at last. His slippers always slowed him up, they were too big for him.

'Clean him up,' said the Charge Nurse, ignoring Henry.

'Rather you than me,' said the policemen, almost in unison. They looked nice and clean and healthy. They swaggered off and disappeared.

Jenny and I walked this Patrick down the corridor to the bathroom. He was no Henry, he put up no resistance.

'What shall we do with his clothes?'

'Don't know, burn them?'

'Can we send them off somewhere, you know, fumigate them?'

'I don't know.'

Patrick groaned. We undressed him. He didn't have many clothes on: nothing at all, beneath his jacket. His trousers stank of fishy old urine, and fleas jumped in the seams. Lice lived beneath the woolly greenish hat. There was a series of big bruises along his skinny back, each knobby vertebra blackened.

'Poor old thing,' said Jenny.

We washed him all over, not fierce with the scrubbing brush

but quite gently, using a special medicated soap to kill off all the bugs. He started to wake up a bit during all this.

I was washing his face again – we had to bath him twice – when he suddenly focussed his eyes on me and spoke.

'Hallo, hen,' said Patrick, and smiled.

I took the flannel away, startled.

'Hallo,' I said.

'Am Ah back here again?' asked Patrick. His accent was very familiar to me. I realized straight away who his voice reminded me of.

'How are you feeling?' Jenny asked, sitting back on her heels.

'Terrible,' said Patrick, sounding cheerful. 'Am Ah back in this bin, eh?'

'It's a bin all right,' I said. We laughed, Patrick laughed, and then slumped very suddenly backwards, so that I had to fling myself towards him to catch him before he cracked his head against the rim of the bath. He seemed to be asleep again.

We got him clean and dry. He looked much better already. He was co-operative throughout, as if he were entranced. We put him to bed, tucked him in.

'He's rather sweet,' said Jenny.

The next day Patrick could open his eyes properly. He had blue eyes, and his beard, freshly soaped, was white and soft. He looked a bit like Father Christmas, Santa after a nasty bender.

'Hallo, hen,' said Patrick to Jenny.

'Hallo, ma wee birdie,' said Patrick to me.

In two days he was back on his feet again. We had him on Heminevrin and vitamin shots and diet supplements and three meals a day so he was feeling better, if shaky. He came and sat next to me in the dayroom. We talked a little. I gave him a cigarette. His tone and phrasing were so familiar to me that I felt I had to say so, though this seemed rather a risky undertaking somehow. It made my heartbeat quicken to think of it.

Finally, after a pause, I said, 'My father was an exile, too.'

Patrick didn't pick up on the past tense. Well, he was the patient after all.

'Ah haveny been back to Scotland now for twenty-five years,' said Patrick, and he talked about his grandmother, who had kept bees somewhere in the country, in Ayrshire.

'That was a long long time ago,' said Patrick.

'Patrick's doing well,' I volunteered a week later at report. 'He wants to stay clear, he wants to try Antabuse.'

'Again?' murmured the Charge Nurse.

'It's a waste of time,' said the Staff Nurse. He was a Cockney Asian, bored into lethargy. When I'd first arrived on Hardwick ward I'd asked him lots of increasingly shrill questions: Why was so much ECT done? Why didn't the patients have anything to do? Why were we making Mhairi stay alive? Why wasn't Henry transferred to a proper geriatric unit? His answer to all these: 'It's the system.'

'It's a waste of time,' said the Staff Nurse now.

'But we've got to try!' I cried. I heard myself, all squeaky eagerness.

'Yes,' said the Charge Nurse, composedly. I looked away.

So Patrick was written up for Antabuse. I doled them out with pleasure.

'See that,' said Patrick, taking his medicine. 'Ah'm gonty stay clear this time. Get maself a place. This is it, for me.'

He seemed cheerful. I felt better too. I had managed to get him a place at a hostel on his impending release. I'd prodded the bored Staff Nurse into arranging a social worker's visit for him. Using a DHSS booklet I explained how he could go about getting social security while he looked for a job. He had once, he told me, been a printer.

'But Ah couldny cope with that now,' said Patrick. 'A wee job in the country, that's what I'd like, odd-job man on a farm eh, something like that. Ah could do something like that.'

Every day he sat next to me in the dayroom. He sought me out.

'You're sympathetic. Ah can talk to you.' And he would talk for hours. I knew what his mother had liked best for breakfast, I knew his favourite colour. I knew the complete geography of the Ayrshire farm. When he'd finished all his stories he began to tell them all again, and again.

I would smile, and look out of the window. By now I only had a week more to go on Hardwick ward. One week more, and then I would be free. Besides, I felt by this time that I'd misjudged Hardwick, made a fuss when no fuss was really necessary. It had certainly been an unpleasant ward-experience, I told myself, but it was really nothing salutary or of vital and terrible significance. I'd over-reacted, that was all.

And there was only a week to go. I felt almost relaxed, even there, sitting in the dayroom where the air smelt so of scorching. Almost relaxed. I smiled. Patrick thought I was smiling at him.

'Ma wee birdie,' he said.

Things went all wrong just after that.

A nurse came down from Bennett ward the following day.

'We need a hand please,' she told our bored Staff Nurse. He didn't ask why. He sent Jenny and me. I felt glad enough to go, I'd spent the last hour wrestling with Henry. We followed the Bennett ward nurse up the stone staircase. We all three had our arms folded, I noted nervously. Already I could hear faint hoarse screams, there was a woman screaming on Bennett ward.

'We need help holding her down,' said the Bennett ward nurse, pausing outside the door, 'so's we can give her her Largactil.'

'Oh,' I said helplessly. The screams suddenly amplified as she swung open the heavy broad door.

We went in. A little knot of people were all crammed into one corner of the women's dormitory, crouched over or kneeling beside the woman who was screaming. She lay on her back, half under one of the beds, which had been pushed askew. Some of her screams were in blurred gurgling words:

'Naw, naw, I don't want it, nah!'

Her face was very red, and her tight dress had ridden up over her big bare thighs.

'She's been really hyper all morning,' shouted the Bennett ward nurse over the screams. She took a step forward, towards the little struggling group in the corner. 'Sister! I'm back!'

At this a small hunched middle-aged woman looked up from the corner, saw Jenny and me, and quickly rose. She looked very angry. She was holding a metal kidney bowl with a needle and loaded syringe in it. It clinked as she hurried towards us.

'For goodness sake!' she hissed furiously at the Bennett ward nurse, 'I mean for goodness sake nurse! We need muscle here, not more women, we need muscle!' She tapped at the kidney bowl with her fingernails. There was a red mark, a clear knuckle print, over her left cheekbone.

'Oh I'm sorry, Sister,' said the Bennett ward nurse, looking agonized. 'Shall I —'

'Go back to Hardwick, tell them what we want and why, all right?'

'No no no no *no*,' screamed the woman on the floor, trying to writhe. 'Yes, Sister,' I said.

'I don't know, for goodness sake,' muttered the Sister, turning her back.

Jenny and I scurried away, pursued by the patient's yells.

'I don't want it, I don't want it – '

I pulled Bennett's heavy door shut behind us. I breathed out; I seemed to have been holding my breath for some time. We went downstairs again.

'Crumbs,' I said, catching Jenny's eye. She went red and said straightaway, 'It's disgusting!'

'Well,' I said, rather abashed, 'I suppose they only want to make her feel better.'

'So bloody what!' said Jenny. Her eyes filled with tears. 'Bennett's not a locked ward. That woman wasn't sectioned, she's a voluntary patient! So she can say no, and it's illegal to force drugs into her, it's an assault.' We reached Hardwick's door and stopped. Jenny lifted her glasses and rubbed her eyes.

'So that means – '

'They wanted us to assist in a *crime*!' said Jenny.

I looked at her. Was it the assault, or our near-involvement in it, that had made her cry? I remembered the Charge Nurse kicking the ex-patient, and that I had told no one about it, not even Jenny. I felt a small quiver of guilty panic run all over me.

'Should we say something?' I asked her.

There was a long pause.

'I suppose it wouldn't change anything,' she said at last.

'No.'

'Just cause a lot of trouble.'

'Yes.'

Another pause.

'She was being a bit violent, I think,' I said.

'Well, she's not our patient.'

'No.'

Pause.

I opened Hardwick's door. 'And we've only got a week more to go,' I said.

'Yes, thank God . . .'

We went inside, and found the bored Staff Nurse.

'Oh well,' he said, stretching in the office, 'I suppose I'd better get up there then.' He smirked. 'Help all those little ladies out.' He closed the door behind him, and turned to me.

'You know your Patrick's gone?' he asked.

'What?'

'Done a bunk. Run off. He always does.' He smiled down at me. 'Told you.' He sauntered off towards the staircase.

I pressed my hands over my mouth.

'Tell you something else,' called the Staff Nurse from the door, 'he wasn't taking the Antabuse. Pile of it in his locker. Could have told you.' He disappeared.

'Come on,' cried Jenny, pulling at my arm. I have a confused memory that she actually grabbed me by the lapels as well but that can't be right. 'Come on,' she cried, 'we'll get him back!'

'What?' I said again. The air suddenly felt quite different all around me, it felt like some different medium altogether, something like water.

'Patrick, we'll get him back, he can't have got far.'

'But we can't!'

'Why not?'

Because he's not sectioned either, I might have replied, had I been able to breathe real air. As it was I could only come up with: 'We can't just leave!'

'Don't see why not. Come on. Just to talk to him, that's all. I mean, that's all, come on!'

We got our coats on, picked up our bags from the empty office.

'All clear?'

I peeped up and down the corridor.

'Okay!'

We walked quickly down the path. We kept bumping into one another.

'Don't look so furtive,' said Jenny, between anger and the giggles.

We stood beside the main road in front of the hospital. The traffic made a bright loud roar. I felt a bit dazed, as if I'd just come out of a matinee at the pictures, and found that it was still daylight after all. There were non-mad people everywhere, pushing prams and carrying shopping bags.

'Half an hour,' said Jenny. 'I'll go this way, right?'

'Right.'

We parted. I set off. After a few minutes I began to feel angry with Jenny. This was all her fault. Here I was playing truant, and it was all her fault. I lit a cigarette and stumped along, puffing crossly. There was a cold wind blowing, it tangled my old woollen skirt against my legs as I walked. I stopped to pull it free, and noticed a broad, long ladder in my tights, along my shin. I wondered if I looked like an escaped mental patient. What am I doing this for? I asked myself, and instantly felt so horribly panicked that I stopped in my tracks, to catch my breath.

As I stood there I noticed a little park on my left. I walked up to the gates and looked in. The grass was thin and flattened, as if too many feet had trodden on it. There was a bench there, set beside an empty flower-bed. Sitting on the bench, looking at me, was Patrick.

I threw my cigarette butt down and stood on it. I thought that if I seemed unhurried Patrick would not be frightened. I mustn't frighten him, I thought. Slowly I walked up to him. I smiled.

'Hallo there.'

'Hallo, hen.'

'I sit down?'

'Please yourself,' said Patrick. He sounded neutral, neither friendly nor unfriendly, not even very surprised. I sat rather stiffly down beside him, and gave him a cigarette. I lit myself another, with some difficulty as the wind was still blowing.

'You come after me?' asked Patrick after a pause.

I nodded ashamedly. Patrick smiled, and shook his head.

'I was hoping you'd come back,' I said, with embarrassment. It felt rather like trying to chat someone up at a party, someone who clearly wasn't interested.

'What's the point,' said Patrick.

'You were getting better.'

'It wis just – a dream,' he said. His voice was light with what sounded like fake wistfulness. I turned to look at him. Patrick heaved a great sigh. 'Ah'm just fit for the gutter,' he said.

It took me a second or two to swallow this. I moved my feet

about, making a gritty sound on the concrete path. Then I went on trying, God knows why.

'You were going to get a place,' I said.

Patrick sighed and tutted, but his face had changed; he looked bored, irritable. Unhurriedly he stood up, and I saw the little bottle in his jacket pocket: rum, probably. I stood up too, and faced him, shaking with a sort of excitement.

'Why did you lie to me?'

Patrick stretched his neck about. It had all been just his little joke, I thought, just some private half-conscious joke he'd been playing on Authority, which was all I had been to him.

'Why did you bother?'

'Ah'm off,' he said.

'You stay here,' I shouted. I felt rage move in me, strong as arousal. I felt its power.

'You stay here!'

He looked up at me. I saw his little eyes, I saw contempt in them, contempt for me, in his little half-human eyes.

'No!' I cried, and raised my hand. I raised my hand.

'Fuck off,' said Patrick.

I raised my hand, and the doors of hell swung open. Truth lay behind them, truth like napalm.

I hit Patrick. I struck his cheek. I struck Mhairi and the tongue-less Bengali, and the bored Staff Nurse and Henry, I struck the drug trolley and the ECT machine, I struck the padded cell and the straitjacket, and all the pain in all the world that I didn't want to see.

'Yes, yes,' said Patrick.

Then I went home.

Jenny told them I'd gone off sick. I told Jenny that I hadn't found Patrick.

'Neither did I,' said Jenny. 'It was a mad thing to do anyway. I don't know what came over me.'

'No,' I said.

This all happened years ago now. I did a gastro-enterology ward after Hardwick: cancers and bowel surgery; I was soon feeling better. From later students I heard, from time to time, news of some of the patients I had known on Hardwick ward.

Henry was sent to a long-term psychogeriatric hospital outside London. Perhaps he is dead by now. Mhairi is. She seemed to get better, and was allowed home to her family for a weekend; she hanged herself in her mother's bedroom.

The Bengali lady recovered, and went home holding her husband's hand, smiling. Her speech was a little thickened, it seemed, but that was all. It was mysterious: she was well.

The last I heard of Patrick, he was on Bennett ward. Perhaps they made sure he took the Antabuse there.

I've tried to forget it all, as far as I can. It was the play that reminded me: *Hamlet*, at the Barbican. There are lots of mad people in Shakespeare, but they're not very Hardwickian. That's somehow what reminded me. We'd have held down young Hamlet, I thought, and shot him full of Largactil, Good *night*, sweet prince . . . ECT for Lady Macbeth, I thought, and Lithium for King Lear.

It was a painful sort of joke. It stopped me seeing the play properly. I couldn't finish the lemon ice-cream either. I was thinking about Hardwick instead, and finding that my real difficulty now is that I can't see any alternative.

People will go mad, and madness is pain, I learnt that much. But what can you do with them, except look after them, in case they get better? They just might get better, the Bengali lady did. And if you're going to look after them, you've got to herd them together, organize them, and if you do that, you get Hardwick.

There must be places like Hardwick all over the country and all over the world, some better, some worse, but all potentially places where the nursing staff can go mad along with the patients, or turn into bored small-time Nazis, or do both.

But what else is there to do? People go mad, and madness is pain. We can't just leave them to it.

Can we?

Could you?

Could you stand by, and watch Ophelia drowning?

THE PRODUCTS
OF CONCEPTION

IN JANUARY my flatmate moved out to live with her boyfriend. I was glad about it on the whole. We'd stopped being close friends months before, mainly because I didn't like the man, and because she herself had changed, it seemed to me; stifling her particular self the more to accommodate and resemble him

If I'd fancied him myself I could perhaps have forgiven him for being so infectiously dull, but he didn't appeal to me that way either, being heavy and blunt-featured.

Worse, he was a noisy lover and the flat had thin walls. At night I could hear everything, the giggles and groans, the rhythms, the gear-changes, the final high-speed pounding. Sometimes it seemed as if her bed might come crashing right through the bedroom wall like a loaded battering-ram. I'd wear my old night-duty ear-plugs, I'd put the pillow over my head, I'd turn the radio on.

Of course after a while I began to suspect them. I began to imagine that at least part of their noisiness was exaggerated, so that they would be sure that I would hear them. I began to imagine her imagining me; at some brief point during their love-making, I felt, she would be thinking not of herself nor of him but of me, alone in my single bed, scarcely four feet away, listening in; because my aloneness was an added pleasure to her.

I was ashamed of myself for thinking this but also convinced that it was true. So we couldn't be close friends anymore.

I had planned to re-decorate when she had gone but somehow I never got round to it. I bought a new lampshade for the living-room but that was all I did. I was only lonely sometimes, most often when there was nothing interesting on the television and I'd already had a bath and it was too early to sleep. Then I might feel a bit miserable, thinking how nice it would be to have someone to put my arms around. But it never lasted too long.

I was doing agency work then, in all sorts of different places. Every other week or so I'd turn up in a different hospital reception, waiting for a different Sister-in-charge to show me to the changing-room and take me on to the ward.

Hospitals are all different but their changing-rooms are all alike, always crammed with a winding maze of narrow grey metal lockers and dotted here and there with a dusty pair of long-abandoned duty-shoes. I left a pair behind myself once, some-where. They were plastic and uncomfortable, and I forgot them after a night-shift and never went back to fetch them. I expect that they are still there.

In March the agency sent me to a day-care gynae clinic, which meant free weekends and regular day duty. With an occasional night-shift somewhere else I could pay the rent even though the clinic was open only three days a week. So I stayed on.

The clinic was an elderly place, a piecemeal conversion from something else, a workhouse or a lying-in hospital, something old like that, so it had bits of moulding on the ceilings, all blurred with coat after coat of whitewash, and high arched windows. Some rooms had had new, lower ceilings put in, so that the tops of the arches were cut off, giving them a blunt sawn-off look. There were lots of chairs everywhere too, stacked in piles, I don't know why.

The operating theatre was tiny, with a smooth tiled floor, a new low ceiling, and an ancient sterilizer wedged into one corner. I used it as a desk, to fill out path. lab forms on. I nearly always worked in the operating theatre. There were two other regulars, Robert, the anaesthetist and Leo, the surgeon.

Rob sat by the patients' heads, within reach of his anaesthetics trolley, the usual gleaming steel affair all hung about with corrugated tubing and mysterious glass jars, through which the drugging gases flowed. He wore braces on his trousers and had round red cheeks and innocent eyes, which sometimes looked angry; I avoided him then. Occasionally he brought in a paper-back novel and hardly looked up between cases. But usually he was friendly enough, and chatted as he worked, about recent television programmes – he especially liked The Professionals – and about favourite recipes and holiday plans.

Leo was a bit more distant, though he liked to talk about Greece, where he usually took his holidays. He was rather small and grizzled. He had three children, so the clinic counsellor told me one coffee-break, and the eldest had been brain-damaged at birth and lived a vegetative life in a residential hospital in Surrey somewhere.

'Delphi at Christmas,' said Leo, sighing so that the paper mask fluttered over his lips. 'Clean, clear air. Blue sky. Magic.'

My main job in the theatre was to set up the surgical trolleys before each case. The trolleys were of stainless steel, with loose shelves that rattled over the tiled sluice-room floor. I used to wash them down with soap and water, then rub them all over with surgical spirit. Then I'd set a theatre pack, like a big soft parcel, on top of each trolley, cut the strings, open the outer layer, and go off to wash my hands – for five whole minutes if it was the first set-up of the morning.

Each pack's inner wrapping was of dark green cloth. Rubber-gloved I would unfold it, pulling it straight upon the trolley-top like a nice ironed tablecloth. Within, the sterile drapes and the steel tray of instruments, which must all be laid out in correct order. It was a lot like setting a dinner table.

First the linen: the sheet-size drape to cover the patient from breast to pubis, the smaller vaginal piece to tuck beneath her buttocks, and two long bags like bolster cases to shroud each leg decently.

Then the steelware, the glittering cutlery: the towel-clips, their spiked jaws safely closed; the swabs-on-sticks, like rolls of bandage on wands; two long forceps, splay-ended, to grasp the soft meat of the cervix and pull it into view; next, a heavy broad-bladed spatula, to weigh down the fourchette and keep the labia apart; then the long curved uterine probe, marked off to measure the depth of that hidden loaded cavity; finally the metallic row of graduated cervical dilators, numbered and in order, the slimmest first to hand.

When I had finished I would stand well back, checking that everything was correctly placed and tidy, making sure the dilators were evenly spaced. I never quite got used to the look of the dilators. Handling them troubled me, though they were pleasant enough to the touch, smooth and cool, with blunt, rounded ends. Held a certain way they were undisguisedly phallic, but rather jokily so, laid out like that, a line-up of phallic possibilities. It was my amusement that made me uneasy; it hardly seemed proper in such a place.

Whereas the overall task, the cleaning and the ordered setting-out, often gave me a pure domestic pleasure, a sort of house-wifely glow. Theatre nursing's like that: transcendent house-wifery, housewifery writ large, and paid for; obsessive cleanliness justified.

And I liked making everything nice for Leo. I liked Leo. He was a virtuoso of his kind, an artist of abortion, performing between each case's spreadeagled legs with a precise and tender skill.

'See, this is the secret,' he said to me once, as he drew the latest cervix into view, 'gradual dilation.' He pressed in the slenderest dilator, like a long curved darning needle, and left it protruding there.

'Giving it time.' He tapped his rubbered hand upon his lap to show me that time was passing.

'See? Giving it time to dilate, that's the way.' He pulled the slenderest dilator free, and took up the next one.

'It's made to dilate, the cervix is. That's what it's for. We just need – ' gently Leo slid the next size in – 'to give it a chance – ' tapping – 'to do its job. Right?'

'You get some people,' Leo went on, selecting the third dilator, 'get in a real hurry ... ramming 'em in and out. Do some damage. We ... don't want to do any damage. Do we?' he asked, looking at the small gaping cervix in front of him. Its little mouth hung open.

'No we don't,' Leo told the cervix, pushing in a number four.

He was right, I knew. I had seen some abortions as a student, and often the surgeons seemed almost frantic with haste, tearing through a case-list as if they were out to break records, in a run of gynaecological quickies: with none of Leo's delicate surgical foreplay.

When each case had been coaxed to about a number twelve, I would hand over a fresh sterile suction tube and switch on the extractor. This was a small wheeled machine, with snub 1950s curves. It made a loud vibrant hum like a vacuum cleaner. Blood ran at this stage, whoosh, down Leo's suction tube, splashing into the vacuum bottle on the extractor machine, catching every now and then as some larger piece of detritus momentarily blocked the line.

While this went on I would go and see if Rob was in the mood for a chat, or I'd stare out of our sawn-off window, or I'd stay by the ancient sterilizer to label the path. lab forms and write PRODUCTS OF CONCEPTION on the specimen jars. I didn't like to see the blood flow; it upset me, for various uncomfortable reasons.

Of course I just didn't like the sight of it, of induced' miscarriage – well, who would? But worse, I knew I also felt some kind of bitter satisfaction at seeing pleasure, especially sexual pleasure, thus punished; I could easily attribute this to a childhood prejudice, though; even congratulate myself a little for having noticed the nasty stain of it at all.

More disturbing was the slow realization that I was drawing a certain comfort from this daily demonstration of other people's misfortune: that whatever sort of dreary mess I had steered my life into, at least I had not made this particular mistake, been forced to this particular disaster.

It was easy enough to tidy all this away as normal, and neither noble nor particularly ignoble. But there was more, there was a thought that continued to vex me, and of which I was ashamed. It had occurred to me that disaster itself can have life-giving properties, any disaster, even this one.

Once a friend of mine, an ex-flame, had rung me at home to tell me about an accident: practising a little do-it-yourself carpentry the day before, he had run an electric drill right through the palm of his hand. His voice had sound unfamiliar, a strained mixture of despondency and exhilaration. He had laughed a great deal as he talked. I thought about him for a long while afterwards. This friend's life was as directionless as my own; it seemed to me that the accident had provided him, struggling in his featureless sea, with a sudden rock of reality to cling to. An uncomfortable, barren rock, of course, but better than nothing for a little while. The accident had been a real, dateable event for him; the end of my thinking had been, Well, I suppose it's made a change for him . . .

So too, for these women in the clinic, these cases, this endless procession of splayed shrouded legs, the shock of accidental pregnancy had made a change for them, provided them with a comprehensible dilemma to measure their lives with; an entirely female dilemma too, a mark of female identity.

And I have not even that, was the sum of my feelings as I saw the blood flow. Not even that. I could put no name to my own disasters.

It was so unpleasant to catch myself feeling like that, and so unrewarding to work out why, that I found myself wondering once or twice if self-knowledge really is the great goal it's always cracked up to be. This turning to jokiness cheered me up, as if I were shrugging my shoulders at my own dreary introspections and saying, So what? And after all, I would say to myself, someone's got to do it, and if someone's got to do it, why shouldn't it be me? With free weekends too, and regular hours, and a devil I now knew so well . . .

So I went on talking carefully to Rob, or looking out of the window or slowly filling in the path. lab forms: when the blood flowed, I just made sure my eyes were averted. Then I didn't feel anything very nasty at all.

Until one day, during a late morning case, something rather unusual happened.

It was one of Rob's reading days. He was deep in a paperback with a picture of a man cuddling a machine-gun on the cover, and the forms were all filled in, so I was at the window. It was too high for me to see anything much but sky, with a bit of the slate roofing of the derelict factory opposite. There was a pigeon perching there.

Leo called me over.

'Give us a bottle, love, will you?'

I took a formalin jar from the back shelf and unscrewed the lid.

'What is it?'

'Over here,' said Leo, gesturing at his lap. 'It just fell out.' On his knee lay a strange pinkish shape as long as my ring finger. Its arms and legs ended in melted starfish points. Its head was a vague meaty blob. Leo picked it up with his forceps and it dangled between the jaws, limp and dripping, like a drowned worm.

'Abnormal,' said Leo, poking the thing into the formalin jar. 'Dead already. Dead a good while, by the looks.'

I screwed the lid back on and held the jar up to the light. The thing swung up and down against the glass.

'Will you tell her?' I asked.

'Tell who? Oh, her. Oh yes. Certainly. Don't you think? Cheer her up, dead already.'

He turned back to his work, vacuuming out what remained. I labelled the jar. I had felt a shock all over me at his last words, not of horror, but a confusion-shock. How could anyone be glad to hear that her child had been abnormal, dead already?

I thought of all the specimen jars I had sent off in the afternoons to the laboratories, one jar per case, the products of conception. If the lab technicians, fishing in my specimen jars, came across microscopic abnormality, were they cheered up as well?

I imagined two of them, two white-coated lab technicians sitting on tall wooden stools, saying, Hey look at this one, this one's abnormal, probably dead already – with the unconscious and comforting rider, It wasn't our fault, it wasn't even her fault, it's all right, it was *dead already.*

After lunch I usually sat in the staff lounge with a mug of coffee. Everyone had their own mug. It was often quite crowded at lunchtime, since we all ate our sandwiches there, the recovery-room nurses, the family planning lady, the counsellor, Leo, and I. Rob usually went across the road: 'Anyone coming for a swift half?'

There was a kettle for hot drinks and a communal coffee jar. It was dreadful cheap stuff, I was always planning to bring in a thermos instead but I never managed it, for some reason. I often made coffee for everyone, putting Leo's down by his hand.

'Thanks, love.'

On the day of the abnormal foetus the lounge was fairly quiet, I don't know why. I brought Leo his coffee and sat down beside him.

I had a magazine but I didn't read it. I looked at my fingernails and nibbled at the dry flaking cuticles, result of all that trans-cendent housewifery. I thought about bringing in some hand-cream, and instantly by some strange mental sidestep found myself wondering what Leo said when people at parties asked him how he earned his living; what his wife said, questioned by other wives.

Because I was thinking about him I turned automatically to take a quick look at him and he caught my eye and abruptly spoke to me: 'You all right?' he asked.

I was startled, and answered straight away, 'Oh, yes, of course.'

'Good. Right.' He picked his mug up, held it for a moment, then put it down again.

'You seemed a bit upset,' he said.

My heart gave a great pound at this, I don't know why, perhaps simply at the revelation that anything about me was noticeable at all.

'No, well,' I said, 'that abnormal one – '

'-Yes?'

'I'd never seen anything like that before. That's all.' I was telling the truth as well as hiding it; after all it had been a real monster I had seen, if a little one.

'Not uncommon.' Leo shook his head. 'Happens fairly often, in fact.'

But does it cheer you up too? I wanted to ask. I even thought about asking it, which made my heart beat really fast, at my own daring. I drew breath –

'Pity she didn't leave it a bit longer,' said Leo, just in time. 'Then she'd have miscarried. I expect that's what they all want really, a miscarriage.'

He spoke gently, without bitterness. I looked at him as he sat beside me, at his vague dark eyes and the white hair showing above the neck of his theatre blues. I wanted to put my arm round his thin shoulders, not out of pity but out of a sort of affectionate reverence, because he had made so many abortions, committed, some would say, so many murders, and yet did not blame women at all.

Others did, others do: I remembered again the violent haste I had seen in my student days, and felt that I could now understand it; that, while it had something to do with heavy case-loads, it had perhaps more to do with revenge. Leo blamed no one, not even himself, and so, if not exactly innocent, was not guilty either. He was an artist. I liked him.

And so things might have gone on. I didn't put my arm round him, of course. I didn't touch him at all. For a few days afterwards we smiled more than usual when our eyes met, but they did not meet very often.

Then something else happened, because I had stopped chatting to Rob – he was still reading anyway – and begun standing by Leo's shoulder while the blood flowed. I no longer felt ashamed of the way it made me feel, because I had realized that in all practical ways I was as guiltless as Leo: my reactions did no one harm.

It was because I was standing by his shoulder that I saw what I saw.

We were on the last case of the afternoon. The patient was very young.

'Fifteen,' said Rob, reading from her notes. 'Poor little cow.'

As Leo pushed the probe in she bucked on the table like a landed fish. Leo pulled out fast.

'Oops,' said Rob, twiddling with the knobs on his gas machine. 'Right ... go ahead.'

Leo carried on: probe ... dilation ... suction. The blood flowed. I was all right.

'Look,' said Leo suddenly. 'Look at that.'

With his bloodied suction tube, he was pointing at something caught in the drapes in front of him.

'See that?' I still don't know why he made me look.

I saw a foot, a little foot half an inch long, a perfect miniature as if of ivory, not rounded with fat like a baby's but slender, with a long-boned foetal elegance, ending just above the ankle in a jagged bloodless tear. It gleamed like ivory against the dark sterile drapes. It gleamed.

Leo put his hand out, and brushed it, and it fell into the waste bowl on the floor, and was gone.

I don't think I behaved any differently from normal as I cleared up in the sluice-room that afternoon. I had to scrub and re-pack the instruments before I went home; perhaps I made a bit more noise than usual. I don't know. Anyway instead of hurrying off straight away after the last case Leo hung about in the theatre. I don't know what he was doing. Eventually he came up and stood in the doorway.

'Er, could you untie me, d'you think?'

He came in. I dried my hands and he turned round. I pulled at the strings of the theatre gown.

'You're all knotted up.'

'Mm.'

I undid him.

'Thanks.' He pulled the bloodied gown off and laid it in the linen skip. It hung untidily over the edge. I pushed it in properly, ramming it down rather hard, and went back to the sink, where the instruments lay soaking. Leo stood in the doorway again.

"You're all right?' he asked. I didn't feel pleased this time. I felt angry, I felt obscurely that I had been fooled. I turned the taps full on.

'I'm fine.' I swished the instruments about under the running water. They made a live rushing noise, steel instruments in a steel sink.

'You're sure?' he asked. I felt almost dizzy, flooded with real anger like some violent pleasurable drug. I'm all right, go away! I wanted to shout. Leave me alone, go away!

I turned the taps off, and in the quiet said, 'No, I'm all right, thanks. Really.' I sounded quite normal.

'Right.' I heard him sigh. 'Well,' he said. 'I don't know. Someone's got to do it, right? Safe or dangerous, that's the only choice.'

'I know,' I said angrily. I turned round. 'I know that!' I saw his twisted smile. It struck me for the first time that he might as well be a virtuoso, since it was certainly far too late for him to try his hand at anything else. I felt a sudden almost painful pang of my usual housewifely, table-setting glow.

'What do you say,' I asked him, 'when people at parties ask you what you do?'

'Why, what do you say?'

I half-laughed at him. I had not thought to question myself. Then I saw the answer.

'I don't go. I don't go to any parties.'

'What, never?'

'No.'

'That's very sad.'

We were speaking fast now. I leant against the sink because my legs were trembling so much. Already I half-knew what he was going to say next.

'Ah, I was wondering – '

I looked at him.

'I was wondering if we could meet sometime, er, for a drink or something.'

I hesitated, twisting my hands together, looking at my wrists. Now here was another choice: no or yes, safe or dangerous. I saw that it was our shared and conscious guiltlessness that had prompted him. I saw also that, if I had ever imagined disaster as a rock to cling to, here was a great rock looming; sooner or later Leo would undoubtedly be a very great disaster.

A nameable, coherent disaster.

I looked up at him again.

'Would you?' he asked. 'Meet me?'

I went forward and laid my hand on his arm, as he stood there, still in the doorway. He was trembling too, my guiltless Herod.

'All right,' I said, and smiled.

THE QUALITY OF MERCY

ONE DAY last August I was standing in a queue at the building society waiting to make a withdrawal when something very strange happened to me.

It was a sunny day. I'd got up very late and the sky had hurt my eyes when I'd first closed the front door behind me. I felt a bit frowsy in the building society, in that sweetish smell of new nylon carpeting. Everything looked very clean there and the people on either side of the counter were speaking across it in quiet subdued voices, as if they were in church.

I was tired because I'd slept so long. I took my building society book out and looked at the dots that made up the numbers and after a little while the strange thing happened.

For an instant it seemed that there was a great dim noise everywhere, and a sudden change in the light; that the ground had sighed and lolled over under my feet.

For an instant I heard the noise, saw the flickering, felt movement: perhaps through that same hopeful device that tries to protect you from your alarm clock by altering your dreams.

After the instant I understood that all the disturbance was a feeling, in me, because I had stopped believing in things. Everything around me, the building society office and its clean new smell, the other people in the queue, myself, my clothes, my handbag and Woolwich booklet, had all stopped being real, because something in me, some sentinel left in charge to concentrate on making things look real and whole had momentarily stopped thinking, passed out, or gone AWOL.

It was blankness and emptiness that I felt: the great abnormal dark that children fear.

None of this lasted very long. My trembling legs and bucketing heart were real enough, I noted them and felt real again. I looked round and saw that no one was staring at me: whatever had happened had passed unnoticed. Presently it was my turn at the counter and I stepped up and got the money out all right, and then I went outside.

The light was still dazzling. I walked up and down the street looking at the market stalls there, the little girls' frilly dresses and the bras pegged up on strings. I thought of the poor mad people I had looked after on the psychiatric ward, who had perhaps felt that stunning horror and its physical translation all the time, not just for a few seconds as I had but all the time, all the time. I saw how impossible everything would seem if it had to be played against such a backdrop: you wouldn't be able to do anything properly, sleep or work or wash your hair or go out for a drink, you just wouldn't be able to do anything.

I found a fruit stall and bought myself a bunch of rather expensive grapes. It occurred to me as I was handing over the money that I should get myself a steady job, no more short-term agency stuff or unemployment, but a proper responsible job where I'd get to know where everything was kept, and where I'd learn everyone's names and make sure they knew mine. I felt a lot better after deciding on this and caught a bus home considering where and what.

I had an interview at the end of the following week. It was at a hospital I'd done some agency at so I knew it fairly well. It was one of the old places, the sort with turrets, built as if to withstand a lengthy siege, and topped off here and there with bits of curly wrought iron, good tethering places, I'd more than once imagined, for transatlantic airships or hot-air balloons. There was a tiled corridor about a mile long too, on the ground floor: entering at one end you couldn't see the other, all the lines converged completely like an exercise in perspective.

I relaxed as soon as I saw the woman who was to interview me; I knew the job was mine. I'd met her once before when I was doing agency. She'd signed one of my timesheets and told me how nice it was, Staff, to see an agency nurse for once in a proper starched linen cap, and an apron. She'd batted her old eyelids and smiled at me as she spoke.

I'd felt rather a fraud; it was true I was immaculately turned out but I had my own obscure reasons for this. At home I was always washing and ironing things, I used to iron sheets and underwear and teatowels and starch my nursing aprons using old-fashioned hot-water starch. It all took ages but then I had little else to do. I used to put a record on and sing along as I ironed. I was partly aware that all this slavish domesticity wasn't quite natural to me but I didn't want to look into the whole thing too far. So I felt mildly guilty on being complimented about it.

She'd seemed a wistful old thing though, sitting there in her admin office behind a desk, but still wearing the ward nurse's jingling composite breastplate of pens and scissors and shiny hospital badges, so I didn't just smile back, I made a little speech about how much I regretted the passing of the old image, and that I thought nurses had somehow lost some public respect when they'd taken to zip fasteners and throwaway plastic aprons and paper caps.

I'd been sure this would be exactly what she wanted to hear and I'd been right, she'd just lapped it up, and finished by telling me that she hoped I'd work there again as she handed the time-sheet back. I was pleased with her too: just because of her age she'd reminded me of some of the old-school ward sisters I'd known when I was doing my training, the sort who'd reduced me to public tears more than once. And yet here she was now just eating out of my hand. I thought, I wish I'd known then that all you have to do is sound confident and agree with them; still, it was pleasant enough to know it now, and we'd parted almost affectionately, having cheered one another up, if for all the wrong reasons.

Today for the interview she wore a name-badge: E.V. Holloway, I read, squinting at it over the desk. She remembered me; I knew she wanted to take me on, but I could see that all my qualifications made her a little uneasy, suspicious even.

'So you ah took a ah degree in English, Miss Markham?' She was holding the certificate in front of her as she asked.

'And *then* you went into nursing?' She looked down, it seemed doubtfully, at my other documents, GNC, hospital, midwifery certificate, the written references.

No, the whole lot's a forgery, I thought, but mildly. I could see one of the mad Rapunzel towers outside through her office window, and quickly sketched in the looming airship, the old R101, with a basketful of champagne-guzzling sophisticates waving from underneath. I smiled at Miss Holloway.

She was talking about the ward, Mercy ward, my ward: a male medico-geriatric ward, 'A little run down due to ah present ah circumstances – '

I knew exactly how run down the place could be, having worked briefly on its sister-ward, Patience, across the corridor. Besides hospitals usually promote their own, if their own stick around long enough: to advertise the post meant that staff turnover rates must be high. I smiled again and told Miss Holloway that I was especially looking for a challenging job with lots of responsibility, and how unsatisfying agency work had been in both these respects.

She liked this speech too and after a few more on similar lines she stood up and congratulated me and said that she wanted to welcome me aboard; and she called me Sister Mercy.

That was a real old-school touch; not many ward sisters are known by the ward's name these days. You can see why it's died out, when modern wards are called units, and numbered. You couldn't call someone Sister E5, or Sister unit 53. Besides the old way had meaning: it was for the old-school sisters, those starched pre-War dragons, professional maidens married to the job, whose wards were life itself.

Sister Mercy. It sounded rather a joke but still it seemed like safety for someone prone to mad horrors in building societies: better to live for a ward than get put away in one.

'Thank you so much, Miss Holloway,' I said, brightly, 'I shall do my very best.' I meant it, too, of course.

It didn't take me long to settle in. The work and the layout were all so familiar, I'd worked in a dozen similiar places. Though none of them had been mine, as Mercy was. I was in charge of it all: the dingy ramshackle ward itself; the other nurses, short-term agency staff and slightly longer-term students; and the patients.

Mercy was a Nightingale ward, with one side-room partitioned in wood and glass like a greenhouse for isolation cases, a high ceiling, and smooth noisy wooden floors. At one end were my office, the treatment room, and the linen cupboard, this last a stifling walk-in affair, crammed from floor to ceiling with redundant foam pillows, knitted-square blankets all felted into some strange bendy substance like rubbery cardboard, never quite enough smooth white linen, and hardly ever enough pyjama bottoms. Tops we had: no bottoms. The bed-fast were often respectable only from the waist up, on Mercy.

At the far end of the ward stood the sluice-room and the bathroom. Two little hand basins had been plumbed into the walls in the early 1960s; they had sprinkler taps so feeble that no one ever tried to use them more than once. Only one sink, in the sluice, was large enough to take a bowl; the bedpan washer leaked, and broke down about once a month, giving warning before each bout of inertia by lavishly flooding the sluice-room floor; all three commodes had brakes so long defunct that the hinges were black with furry grime; and there was one bath. Twenty-seven patients: one bath.

The beds were all different makes and designs, almost a lesson in design evolution, from the heavy cage-like monster on fixed high legs, which could be tilted only by lifting it onto enormous splintery wooden blocks, to the state-of-the-art fixture with various foot pedals and levers to raise, lower, tilt, or sit up the patient, gently and effortlessly, as we pleased. We had two state-of-the-art-ers, and twenty-five assorted ancestors.

Many of the beds had little plaques set into the wall above the head, to commemorate an endowing charity or benefactor: THE HORACE SPROAT BED or THIS BED DONATED BY THE AMERSHAM ROYAL EXCHANGE AMATEUR OPERATIC SOCIETY 1924 or IN MEMORY OF LADY CONSTANCE MILHAVEN 1919 and so on.

I felt a strong duty to read all these plaques whenever I got close enough, in the same way that you sometimes find yourself carefully reading gravestones in cemeteries; as if there's a sort of immortality attached to leaving names in print or stone, but only if the living take the trouble to read them. There was Lady Constance Milhaven relying on me to carry out my end of the bargain; she wore droopy muslins to curtsey in. And Horace Sproat, who had met his end at the Somme, stood coldly to attention, but with sad Wilfred Owen eyes, while the entire chorus of the Amersham Royal Exchange Amateur Operatic Society, a costumed bunch of flushed immortals, held hands to take their final final curtain, all courtesy of me: so I obliged. Presently I knew all the plaques off by heart. It was my ward.

The staff were harder to learn: they came and went so fast. Once early on I arrived unexpectedly to find my two current students clutching illicit mugs of tea in my office. They leapt to their feet, twin blushes; appalled guilt made them look almost identical, two schoolgirls caught smoking behind the bicycle sheds. I remember how I felt, seeing them, that delicious rush of power: I thought how pleasant it would be to be kind to them, how eagerly they would respond. Besides they worked so hard, twenty-seven patients, one bath.

Or rather, as I used to report clearly to Miss Holloway every month at the Sisters' Meeting, twenty-seven patients, one bath, and no hoist.

A hoist is a little crane, a nice easily-maneouvrable little crane with a seat, for lifting helpless people, swinging them up and over the rim of the bath, and gently lowering them into the water. It's for gerries or new amputees or old strokes, that sort. They usually enjoy it, too, there's a slight element of the funfair about it, swinging through the air on a neat little chair; and one slim nurse can bath a wardful of limp sixteen-stoners without even holding her breath.

Of course it was indefensible that Mercy ward should have twenty-seven patients, and one bath, and no hoist. No one was arguing about it, not even the Health Authority.

'But I'm afraid progress has to be piecemeal under the ah under the ah present circumstances,' Holloway would say every month.

Perhaps it was partly to annoy her that I went on trying. I was always in the minutes:

New Business
1. Sister Markham (Mercy) asked that urgent funding be sought for the purchase of a patient-lifting device for Mercy ward. Miss Holloway undertook to re-state the case for this requisition to the appropriate administrative officers.

But in the previous few weeks Miss Holloway had found me out; caught me swearing in my office and seen me lighting a cigarette in the canteen; she knew I'd thrown out that hallowed geriatric-ward institution, the bath book; she knew I sometimes let my old boys lie in bed past nine in the morning if they wanted to; she knew I was friendly with the equally raffish Sister Patience across the corridor. She also knew I had rather pretty legs, which I liked to cross, sighingly, in front of her while she was monthly Undertaking to Re-state: an underhand weapon, I knew, so small that she could hardly be aware of where the sting came from, but still it was the only sting I could needle her with. I knew she'd never give me that damn hoist. I'd found her out too.

My predecessor on Mercy ward hadn't prised a hoist out of her either.

'They didn't have hoists in her day,' said Phyllis Morgan on

Patience ward one late shift after another Sisters' Meeting, 'so she doesn't see why you should need one now.'

'They didn't have antibiotics either,' I said.

'Or hot water.'

'Or bandages. They had to rip up their petticoats.'

'They had a vocation.'

'They had Miss Nightingale. How *was* Scutari?'

'Magnificent,' said Phyllis happily, 'but it wasn't war. Want a refill?' She was holding the teapot.

'No thanks. I've got to get back.' I looked out of the window. The view from Phyllis's office was the rear view of mine: crossing the corridor was like walking through a mirror. It was a dark afternoon, I saw the Rapunzel turrets looming unlit from behind.

'And my sodding bedpan-washer's on the blink again,' I said, standing up and brushing the crumbs off my skirt.

'I don't know,' said Phyllis. 'Why do we stick it?'

'God knows.'

Of course I knew too. I hadn't forgotten what unreality had felt like, I knew why I needed the job. But I hadn't expected it to work quite so well; I had forgotten what nursing can be. It was true that Mercy ward had no hoist and one bath, but it also had the twenty-seven patients. Twenty-seven strangers, all old: the easiest people in the world to please.

I wanted to be needed, I wanted to be recognized. I tried to learn my patients, as far as I could. I tried to be whatever they wanted me to be.

Once in the October of that year, listening to the radio while I did some ironing (I was doing slightly less ironing by then, it had occurred to me that ironing underwear was rather a pointless thing to do), I heard a programme all about prostitution, vox pop stuff with lots of voices, women's voices. It had ended with someone singing, rather sadly, in time to her own street-walking stilettos:

> If you want to end your cares
> Come along and climb my stairs,
> Love for Sale.

I went on ironing my pillow-case, a tricky flounced thing, and thought that the song had got it wrong, that prostitutes offered sex for sale; it was nurses who sold love. It made me smile to myself, the thought of selling my love. I turned the pillow-case over. Why not sell love, if you couldn't find anyone to give it to; no one was willing to *take* it, anyway.

And it was easy to be tender with my old men. Age had made all of them weak and gentle. It took old Fred Sawby fifteen laborious and vituperative minutes to push his Zimmer frame out to the bathroom. Had he ever struck his wife or bullied his children? They were safe from him now. Had he really fed a machine-gun at the Somme? He couldn't hold a teacup now.

Because they were so old, my old men, they told me stories of their youth. I saw the young men they had been while I tended the great-grandfathers they had become, as if there had been no years in between, no gradual decline, but a sudden step from that world to this. They all remembered a war, old men always have a war to remember. It was the Great War for the oldest ones. They talked history, they remembered events so farcically distant, it seemed to me, that it might as well have been the Trojan wars they'd fought in, or Agincourt.

They remembered being visited in the trenches by Horatio Bottomley, they harboured hatred still for Churchill, for Gallipoli; had landed at Archangel, to destroy Lenin; had suffered frostbite, fighting with the Russian Imperial Army in 1915. And there they lay, each under his little plaque, survivors from another world, talking to me as if they knew me, turning on me eyes that had seen the ships go down off Scapa Flow.

You had to feel privileged, you had to feel reverence, talking to such old age. And I tried to be whatever they wanted in return: respectful and grave, or, if they were still sprung with some masculine cheek, the ghostly shade of their old male force, flirtatious and teasing, to help pretend that the shade still had substance. And yet they weren't relations, but clients: I didn't have to hear the stories over and over again, and I was free at the end of my eight-hour shift.

At night when the yellow lights were lit and shining back from each high window, and the night nurses were settled at the centre desk with their crocheting and *Nursing Mirrors*, I'd stand at the door with my apron folded over my arm and bid all my old men a goodnight.

'Goodnight, gentlemen!'

And those that could reply did so: 'Goodnight, Sister,' or

'Night-night, lovey,' or 'Goodbye, gorgeous!' as they pleased.

It was that differing chorus that made me feel I'd perfected an art.

So it was a rhetorical question Phyllis had been asking me that evening after the Sisters' Meeting: Phyllis loved her old ladies, who remembered the details of special dresses, antique childbirth, scrubbing floors by candlelight, or eating turbot at Simpson's in 1912.

'I don't know. Why do we stick it?'

'God knows.'

But Phyllis knew too, and so did I. Love for sale: price, a small wage, and sanity. Love for sale.

It was at the following Sisters' Meeting, in November, that Holloway told me Mercy ward was to be closed, initially for Christmas, and for an indefinite period afterwards.

'But not, we of course hope, for more than a few weeks,' she went on. Her powdery old face had gone quite scarlet as she spoke. I felt simply panicky, my eyes filled. I looked down and stared hard at her shapeless ankles.

'What about the patients?' asked Phyllis fiercely. 'What about them?'

They were to be split up, disbanded, discharged early, sent all over the hospital to wherever a bed could be found. Some of them were to go to Patience ward, when enough Patience ward old ladies had been shunted elsewhere.

'I'm sure the old folk will enjoy their ah get-together during the festive season,' said Holloway.

I looked up to meet Phyllis's eyes at this. She couldn't believe it either.

'I'm afraid I can't accept that, I can't accept that at all,' she said rapidly. Her voice was trembling with rage. I wished I could feel angry too, instead of just beaten.

'I'm afraid there's no question of acceptance; or, or, of not accepting,' said Holloway, losing control a bit but still enjoying herself. She batted her eyelids. 'It's hardly my decision, Sister Patience, I need hardly tell you that – '

'The old bitch, the old bastard, I could strangle her,' said Phyllis. We were sitting in the pub over the road after the shift had ended. 'Enjoy their get-together, I mean, did you *hear* that –' she gulped at her lager. 'I felt like saying to her, I really nearly said it, You're an old virgin, you're nearly as old as they are, how'd *you* like some strange man in the next bed seeing *you* in your nightie and hearing *you* asking for a bedpan, how'd *you* fucking well like it? The cow.'

I put a finger out and traced a clear path down the frosted side of my glass. I was to be relief sister while Mercy was closed. Relief sister, sent all over the place. No one would know who I was. No one would know my name.

'I'll go crazy,' I said to my glass. 'I'll go crazy, being relief sister.'

'No you won't,' said Phyllis crossly. 'Don't be so wet.'

I put my hand over my eyes. 'It'll kill George. It'll kill him, shunting him about.' George was my present favourite. He was eighty-five, a fragile trembly brigadier, a rare officer among my old men. He'd had his best suit on to come into hospital, red braces to keep his baggy trousers up and cufflinks in his best blue shirt; the cuffs all frayed, and scorch-marks at the shoulder where he'd ironed it himself. He was in the Horace Sproat bed. He might have met Horace. He'd have been the elder.

'Shunting George about.'

I rubbed at my eyes and my fingers came away all black, I'd forgotten I'd put mascara on. I'd only just started wearing it again, so I'd forgotten it.

'I'll look after George,' said Phyllis, 'he'll be all right. Honest.'

I looked at her. I thought for a moment of telling her what had happened to me at the building society, but decided against it.

Phyllis drank some more lager, set her glass down.

'Anyway. Listen, are you coming on Saturday then? You should.'

'Sorry?'

'Saturday. You know. Me and Ben are having that little do. Come on. You said you'd come.'

'Oh, I don't know, I —'

'Oh, come on! I mean it was, how long, eighteen bloody months ago, I bet *he's* not stopping in moping, I mean, eighteen months, you've got to get someone new.'

'I don't want someone new.'

Phyllis picked her drink up, scowling.

'Not unless they're old age pensioners, right?'

'Oh come on, you know it's not like that —'

Phyllis leant back suddenly in her chair, crossing her legs so abruptly that one knee knocked the table, and our drinks shivered. I saw that she felt herself to be surrounded by hopeless inadequacy, Holloway's public, mine private. Did she then regard me as another workplace-problem, something to be discussed with her husband or mentioned in passing to her mother?

'I'm sorry I'm such a trial,' I said.

'Oh give over,' snapped Phyllis.

So we didn't part friends.

Closing the ward took a long time. There was more to do than I'd realized. But it wasn't nearly as awful as I'd thought it would be, partly because I'd convinced myself that we'd be re-opening soon and partly because I'd been given a nice long-term agency nurse, a young man, and he cheered me up. It made a change having a young man about the place. Besides, male nurses nearly always lighten a ward's atmosphere, help to dispel that faint sour odour of feminine self-sacrifice that still pervades much of nursing, plastic aprons and zip-fasteners or no. They're such practised flirts, gay or straight. They get more female attention than anyone outside nursing could possibly imagine, except perhaps doctors, and doctors aren't equals; they give orders, they don't make beds with you.

Being surrounded, swamped, overwhelmingly outnumbered by young women makes male nurses rather pleased with themselves, makes the dullest feel, and so perhaps become, more attractive. No wonder they reach the top so fast; it's women who promote them.

Mike was attractive to start with, as prettily androgynous as a teenybopper idol. I saw straightaway from his badges that he'd trained in the same hospital as I had, which is a bit like two old soldiers discovering they've been in the same regiment. We exchanged the usual names and reminiscences, though we had few in common, since he was so much younger than me: he looked about twenty, though he must've been older than that.

Still, discovering that we'd twice worked on the same wards made us feel like old friends. I suppose I tended to treat him almost as if he were another woman but he didn't seem to mind. When he had blond streaks put in his hair I said to him, 'Mike, your hair! It looks great!' in just the same voice I'd have used to Phyllis, if it had been Phyllis's new look.

She'd called me early in December, after nearly a week's silence.

'Hallo. Sister Markham.'

'Hallo, ratbag. How's the quality of Mercy?'

'Strained,' I answered, as usual. I was surprised at how relieved I felt. 'Phyllis, I missed you.'

'I bet. Come over for tea. If you're feeling sociable.'

She rang off. I went through the mirror at 3.30. We ate cream buns supplied by some old lady's relative and groused about Miss Holloway, it was all very satisfying.

'Your young Michael's a bit of all right, isn't he,' said Phyllis.

'He's very sweet,' I said. I lit a cigarette. Phyllis pulled a face at me. 'And he works hard too,' I said. It was lovely doing lifts with Mike. He'd had a good training like mine, he knew how to do a proper Australian lift; that very afternoon we'd lifted frail George right up his bed without hurting him at all, Ooh, that's *much* better, George had said, smiling: sometimes nurses don't know how to lift properly, you end up hauling people about by hooking the crook of your elbow under their armpits, and that hurts them.

'I suppose he's got to be gay,' said Phyllis, 'looking like that. Is he?'

I laughed. 'How on earth should I know?

'Well he wears earrings doesn't he. Don't know how he gets away with it, we couldn't even wear sleepers, let alone a bloke doing it – I mean, what does Holloway say?'

'She's all over him,' I said, realizing that this was so. 'She makes eyes at him.'

Phyllis wrinkled her nose and giggled. 'Yuk. Horrible old bag.'

I felt confused at this: that Phyllis thought it suitable for me to see Mike's charm, but unsuitable, disgusting even, for Holloway to see it too, as if there were some line she'd crossed, of age, or possibility. When would I cross it myself, and would I know it when I had?

'How's the closing going?'

'Oh, we're getting there. Half empty already.' We were

emptying all the cupboards too. I'd discovered one I'd never seen before, inside the linen cupboard, behind a box of plastic-covered foam pillows. It had taken me twenty minutes to find a key that fitted. I had to stand on a chair to reach it and I nearly fell off it once I'd got the cupboard open, out of sheer surprise, because it had been crammed full with boxes of chocolates, stacks of them, all different, some in pretty wrapping paper. There were two bottles as well, one of wine, the other of sherry. An earlier Sister Mercy had clearly followed the old policy of locking away gifts from patients and relatives for special occasions, usually for a Christmas glut. Perhaps she'd forgotten this hoard. Everyone else had. The chocolates were inedible, every single boxful, the sweets all white and shrunken with age.

I'd handed them down, box after box, to Mike, who'd stuck his head out of the linen-room and shouted Treasure trove! at my one remaining student, but there was nothing to share out after all. I put the bottles in my office cupboard, and thought that I'd give all my last old boys a little drink on their final day on Mercy, if their doctors didn't object.

I told Phyllis about the chocolates and she told me how she'd recently come across a battered old cardboard box stuffed darkly away on Patience, and opened it to find three large pieces of heavily boned and studded elastic labelled 'One-size surgical corsetry' and how, in a quiet moment, she and two students had buckled and hooked one another into these objects, though nearly helpless with laughter, and how, encased and tearful, one-sized surgical corsets straining over their aprons, they had looked up to discover a particularly stuffy old consultant standing pop-eyed at the office door.

I was still grinning when I got back to Mercy ward. Mike was sitting at the centre table, writing the kardex. The student, Janet, was playing cards with George and Terry Sullivan, who was technically young for Mercy but had drunk himself as old as George.

I sat down beside Mike.

'We could do the curtains when you've finished?' I asked.

'Yeah ... all right.'

I looked at him, at the curve of his cheek and his long eyelashes, at his hand as he wrote. Had George's hands once looked like that? It seemed impossible that Mike might ever grow as old as George. I thought that if he did there wouldn't be a war for him to talk about, because if there was a war now there'd be no survivors to remember it. Perhaps there would be no war; perhaps there would be a new thing in the world, a whole set of old men who'd never been soldiers.

'Oh, something I meant to tell you, something you'll just love to hear,' said Mike suddenly, sitting back.

'Oh?'

'You did agency here, didn't you, did you ever work on A3?'

This was in the new wing, far along the mile of tiled corridor.

'A3?' I thought. 'No.'

'Aha. Well I did. I did two shifts there last month. It's ENT, kids mostly, or young adults getting tonsils, right?'

'Yes?'

'Yeah it's all spanking new, all the sink units match, you know, everything works, and, I just remembered it today, *and*' he grinned at me, '*and* they've got a hoist.'

'What? You're kidding.'

'Nope. They've got a beautiful new bathroom and they've got a hoist. Never used of course – '

'Isn't it just typical – '

'Yes, kids and young adults. So they get a hoist. Well, because it's all new, I suppose they think, well, get it all right to start with – '

'Oh, I can't believe it, the times I've asked – '

'Mm. I suppose they'll get here eventually, you know, work their way along the corridor up this end, do up this end as well.'

'But under the ah the ah present circumstances,' I said, batting my eyelids, 'it'll be sometime in the next five hundred years,' Mike finished. We smiled at one another.

'Are you upset about it closing, I mean, are you out of a job?'

'No, not really. I was upset at first. I've got used to it. I'll miss my old men though.'

'Yeah,' Mike nodded.

'When I started my training, what, ten years ago,' I said, 'I did a geriatric ward then, and all the old boys were Victorian, they were all, you know, nineteenth century. It was *all* the First World War they'd been in. They're dying out now, old people are nearly all Edwardians now.' It felt a little risky saying this, but Mike said, 'I like it when they talk about the war, all those things you read about. I suppose there'll be more Edwardians, 'cos more of them missed the war, they didn't get killed off like the Victorians, like Horace Sproat, poor old Horace.'

I felt very pleased with him. 'You read the plaque,' I said.

'Yeah, Horace Sproat. What a name, eh, Horace Sproat.'

'Fred Sawby was at the Somme.'

'I know. So was my great-grandad actually. He got gassed.'

'I suppose it seems romantic because it was so long ago?'

'Fred Sawby's not romantic.'

I giggled. Then I said: 'No; he didn't get killed. If he'd been killed he'd have been one of those white crosses, those poppies in November. He'd've been in all that poetry –'

'Half the seed of Europe, one by one,' said Mike, and I was so pleased I touched his arm with delight.

'Oh, I thought of Wilfred Owen when I saw Horace's plaque, poor Horace –'

We talked about poetry we remembered while we unhooked the heavy blue curtains round the empty beds and folded them up for cleaning. The ward looked even emptier without them.

Then it was suppertime. Messages about our depletion hadn't reached the kitchen yet, they were still sending us enough food for twenty-seven, tonight a huge Dickensian steak-and-kidney pie – you don't get individually wrapped plastic trays in hospitals with mad Rapunzel towers on. There are occasional advantages, you understand. The pie looked lovely, I cut everyone huge wedges and there was still enough for Janet and Mike and me. Janet went to the canteen anyway to meet a friend of hers who was undergoing an extremely complicated personal crisis, according to Janet's lurid and enjoyable reports, and Mike and I sat in the kitchen, talking and eating the leftover gooseberry tart while the patients drank their tea.

We'd barely finished when the night nursing officer came round, reconnoitring. He was a big blond man, he came into the kitchen and hung about chatting for a while. I don't think he even glanced at me, not once.

'Well, must be pressing on,' he said eventually. At the door he turned and wished me goodnight, but he was still looking at Mike.

As soon as his footsteps had died away we met one another's eyes and burst out laughing.

'Well, you have made a conquest,' I said.

'Happens all the time,' said Mike, mock-despairing, his hand to his forehead.

'He'll be asking you out tomorrow,' I said.

'I'll be busy,' said Mike, a little cool. I felt abashed.

'Shall we do some backrubs?'

'Okey-doke,' said Mike.

There was seldom a lot to do at that time of day but there was even less now we were half-empty. Everyone left seemed half-asleep as well, too much pie perhaps. No one wanted anything. After the late drug round we sat down at the centre table to wait for the night staff. I was wondering about Mike, whether he was unhappy about being gay, whether it had been a sort of sexual politeness in him to hint to me that he was straight, because to be outright gay is to tell a woman that you're never going to find her the least bit attractive. I looked covertly at his filmstar eyelashes and he turned and faced me and said in rather a low voice, so that Janet didn't hear, 'Coming for a drink after?'

'Oh, I can't tonight, I can't thanks,' I said, all flustered. Then I thought I'd make a joke of it. 'D'you always ask your ward sisters out?'

'No,' said Mike laughing, 'they usually ask me.'

Ten days later we closed the ward: the end of Mercy. Mike opened the wine for me and we gave all the remaining old men an inch each. Everyone's bed was loaded with belongings in bright yellow plastic bags. George lay in bed holding his slippers, waiting to be wheeled away. He was going to Patience.

'Goodbye, George. I'll come and visit you.'

'Goodbye, my dear,' said George. I tried to imagine him barking orders, inspiring terror in the ranks. I kissed his slack cheek.

'Take care of yourself.'

One by one we shunted them out, porter at one end, nurse at the other. They were all gone by lunchtime. We pushed the few remaining empty beds to one side, for the floor cleaners. No beds, no bed curtains.

'It looks like a deserted ballroom,' said Mike, looking round. Our footsteps sounded very loud on the wooden floors. Once, to save time the month before, I had bowled the ward keys along the boards to Janet, who'd wanted them at the far end of the

ward, and she had stopped them neatly with her foot, winning
an ironic patter of applause from the old boys nearby.

'Howzat!'

'We'll finish the cleaning after lunch,' I said. 'Come on.'

It was slow going. I was feeling so miserable that I infected the
other two, and we cleaned the sluice-room almost in silence.

'You know what we should do,' said Mike suddenly,
straightening up from the commode whose nasty jammed brakes
he'd been listlessly poking at, 'we should go out in a blaze of
glory, that's what we should do.'

I was re-lining the urine-testing cupboard. I'd found broken
glass in it, from a smashed dropper, and three bottles of Labstix,
all empty. Janet had disappeared altogether, in search, she'd
said, of rubber gloves, because the Glitto was hurting her hands.

'That's what we should do.'

'How d'you mean?'

Mike looked round, and came closer. 'A blaze of glory. Yes?
We steal the hoist.'

'What?' I turned round, laughing.

'Look. They don't need it. They don't use it. A3. We need it,
they don't.'

'We're shut.'

'Not for long. Come on. We'll get it and then it'll be there for
when you re-open.'

He pulled himself up to sit on the draining board. 'What d'you
say?'

He sounded serious. So did I: 'It's the most idiotic thing I ever
heard.'

'No, no, think about it. Really. It's not stealing really. It's
borrowing. We go up there and we say, Look, we need this hoist
and you don't, can we borrow it, you get it back if you need it.
They won't mind.'

'Oh yes? What about Holloway?'

'What about her? She won't even notice, when did she last
look in your bathroom? She never does, why should she?'

'She won't like it.'

'She won't know. Anyway who cares what she wants, she
doesn't care about you lot does she, all your students hurting

their backs, honest it's half-killed me working here and I'm a bloke!'

I bit my lip, staring into the urine-testing cupboard. Its wooden doors were all blotched with stains, I wondered what of.

'Come on,' said Mike, leaning towards me, his mouth close to my ear. 'Let's do it. Take it. Go on. Dare you.'

It was very difficult trundling the hoist along the mile of corridor. It wasn't built for long distances, it had awkward little wheels and kept trying to knock itself out against the tiled walls. We'd had a terrible struggle getting it in and out of the lift because the wheels stuck in the lift-door grooves and because we were laughing so much. It had a noble, pained look to it, that hoist, like a statue of some long-dead dignitary being knocked off its pedestal by a proletarian mob.

'Listen you bastard you're coming with us,' Mike had snarled, fighting it into the lift beside A3 while the A3 Sister looked on and giggled. Everyone had been full of the Christmas spirit on A3. The Sister had a piece of tinsel tied round her hospital badge in a bow. She'd been surprised at first, then amused, then eager to co-operate.

'Oh, Holloway, oh *her*. Take it, take it, why ever not?'

'See?' Mike had said, smiling sweetly at the A3 Sister, 'I told you they'd be nice.' He'd done nearly all the talking: he'd soon beat all the quick-promotion records, I'd thought rather sourly, my eyes on the A3 Sister's answering smile.

Now, stubborn unco-operative hostage, the hoist fought back as we panted up the last quarter-mile of corridor. There were crowds of people about because it was visiting-time but it's a common enough hospital sight, two people struggling fiercely with an awkward wheeled appliance, so no one stopped us, not even the big blond nursing officer who saw us from the door of admin; he merely smiled tenderly as Mike waved.

'Afternoon!' called Mike. We trundled past, red-faced.

'Ha!' said Mike as we reached Mercy's cramped little bathroom. 'Blazor glory!'

'Oh God, it won't fit,' I cried, anguished. Janet ran up to help us squeeze it past the doorjamb. It fitted, just. Janet instantly sat in the swing and we turned the wheel, lifted her, and, 'God bless all who sail in her,' said Mike, lowering Janet slowly into the empty bath. She sat there grinning till I put the plug in and turned the taps on, when she leapt out squawking.

'And we keep the door closed,' I said as I turned the taps off. 'Keep quiet about this, all right?'

'Right.'

'Come on, let's celebrate, there's some wine left,' said Mike, and we all went into the office and toasted the quality of Mercy, which was, I said, undeniably improved.

'And soon to re-open by popular demand,' said Mike. 'All those Edwardians.' Our eyes met, at that.

Then Janet's friend, the personal-crisis one, arrived and looked pleadingly into the office. It was quite late anyway and there were no late-shift nurses to give report to and no patients to report on, so I told Janet and Mike they could go home if they wanted to.

'I liked working here,' said Janet to me as she left. I thanked her and said I'd enjoyed having her, which she knew already from signing her ward report.

I turned back into the empty ward. It was getting dark already outside. I switched the main lights on. The little plaques looked down on nothing, no beds, no patients. There was no glad end-of-term feeling about it at all, despite the hoist and the blazor glory; it felt more like the end of the world.

'Deserted ballroom,' said Mike behind me. 'Care to dance?'

'I don't feel like dancing.'

'You're a barrel of laughs you are. Come on. Dance with me.'

'I can't dance.'

'You can waltz. Everyone can waltz.'

'I can't.'

'I'll teach you,' said Mike, 'look, it's easy, a waltz. Right, forward, side, together, right, one, two, three, forward side together – I mean, back, side together. Go on.'

'Back, side, together?'

'Right, see? Easy.' He took my hand, I put the other on his arm. We looked at our feet and moved off awkwardly.

'One two three.'

'Back, side, together.'

Mike began to hum the Blue Danube and we lurched about laughing, I kept tripping up unless I kept my eyes on my feet. Still, the ward was a big place to practise in and by the time we'd reached the bathroom and turned to come back down it felt more

like dancing, more like that special metaphor. I remembered waltz-
ing at school then, a hallful of girls all dancing with each other.

Mike put his arm round my waist.

'Aren't you little,' he said. I looked up, he wasn't much taller
than me. There was dark stubble on his chin; it contrasted rather
nicely, I thought, with the dyed blond hair. He looked very raffish,
the gold earrings glinting in the oblique light from the office.

'All those nurses asking you out,' I said.

'Such a burden,' he smiled.

'Women too?'

'Women mainly, dear,' said Mike, rather camp. 'Because I'm
gentle, see,' he went on in his real voice, 'I'm never a threat. I look
effeminate, and gentle.'

'Are you really so, then, or is it an act?'

'Oh well . . . No, I was gentle and effeminate to start with. But
when I saw, you know, how it *worked* . . .'

'Slays 'em?'

'Every time. You know, when I first started nursing, well! I was
in heaven. I was just in heaven: all those girls!' and he smiled
down at me, not lasciviously, but happily, remembering delight.

'How old are you?'

'Twenty-three. How old are you?'

'Thirty-one.'

We smiled at one another, we stopped dancing.

'There. Now we've got that out of the way. Look. Can't I see you
again?'

'What's the point?'

'Lots of point, I think. This ward. It'll be us one day, won't it?
The Elizabethans.'

We moved off again, no music. We danced past the plaques,
Horace Sproat long gone, the Amersham chorus all silent now,
Lady Constance gone to dust.

'Lots of point,' said Mike. His eyes were very gentle. As he
knew.

I thought of the past and going mad in building societies, and of
how much simpler and safer it was to sell love rather than give it
away. Then I smiled into his white coat, where he wore a hospital
badge just like my own. I put my hand on his shoulder.

'Actually,' I said, 'I know how to polka. We learnt it at school.
Shall I show you how?'

THE DRY
FAMILIAR PLAINS

ONE QUESTION I often ask people (by which I mean men, it's a courting question) is whether, as children, they ever set anything on fire.

I can remember being a little nervous the first time I asked this, but the response was reassuring and in fact almost every man I've asked since has laughed and admitted to some small arsonical disaster: grandmother's bed ('I tried to put it out using the toothmug from the bathroom, then I stood at the top of the stairs and called to my mother, I called *Mum* in, what? four syllables? you know, *Ma-a-a-am* ... God her face belting up those stairs); a tidy length of privet hedge ('I was playing at burning up the dead bits in the middle, suddenly whoosh the whole bloody thing's on fire, flames eight feet high all round the garden, whoosh') and Philip, I remember, had been involved as a teenager in a handbag fire, when his girlfriend, nervous at tea-time in her parents' house, had playfully swung her small suede handbag at his head, and a box of matches inside had ignited all at once at the contact; the girlfriend's mother, leaping up screaming at the smoke, had knocked over the occasional table, splashing Philip's ankles with scalding tea and sending all her own best tea-set scudding in bits across the parquet.

I hadn't been quite satisfied with this one, I'd probed a little: 'No, I meant, when you were a child. I bet you did. Men always have. Come on. Own up.'

And then he had remembered, one of the best stories of all, it seems to me: he remembered boredom on a cultural foreign holiday, a cool summer evening in a tall Spanish guest-house, and flying paper aeroplanes out of a top bedroom window to swoop and pirouette down to the courtyard below; later he had set each one on fire, to trail smoke and consume themselves as they flew, spiralling in flames through the still blue air.

'It looked so pretty ...'

The last one disappearing neatly and inevitably and still in glittering flames into an open second-storey window.

'I thought my heart would stop –'

'How old were you?'

'Ten. I just stood there waiting for the smoke and flames to start. For about an hour. But nothing happened. I suppose no one was in, nothing happened.'

I saw an uneasy footsore tourist pausing on his threshold to sniff at the carbon tang of the air, scratching perhaps at scorchmarks on the carpet or puzzling over a singed geranium.

'Anyway, why d'you ask? Have *you* ever set anything on fire?'

'Girls don't set things on fire. My brother did though. He set my bedroom curtains on fire – '

Not on purpose, of course. It was an accident.

'I didn't mean to,' Timmy had wailed, loitering weepily on the landing when the flames and the fuss had all died down, 'it was an accident.'

Everyone else says that too.

('Why though? Why did you do it?'

'Well. I don't really know. I didn't mean to.'

'But you must've known, you must've known that if you touched off the eiderdown the whole bed'd go up?'

'No, no, I sort of, I wanted to see what would happen, I didn't really think anything would happen. I don't think I did. I don't know. I can't remember. It was an accident.')

The day that Timmy had his accident with my bedroom curtains was also a day when my father lost his temper with me: I'd asked him about the dollshouse again and he'd spoken very sharply and said he would get *round* to it for God's sake, and to stop going on and on and on about it. Then he'd said he was sorry, in the same voice, and put his hand over his eyes.

I'd known it hadn't been a good time to ask, what with my bedroom curtains in yawning tatters round the window and half the wall all sweaty black, but something had made me ask. I really wanted the dollshouse. And he'd promised to build me one.

'But you promised,' I wailed, and I was so frightened at being impelled to say this, knowing all the time that it was the wrong thing to say, that it would make him even angrier, that I began to cry as I said it, and he got up very quickly and walked right out of the house, banging the kitchen door so hard behind him that things on the draining board jumped and rattled.

That night my mother came into my bedroom and hung an old bedspread over the window, hammering in tin-tacks with the heel of one of my father's shoes. She hardly spoke to me. She seemed to be blaming me about the curtains, which I thought was unfair. I lay in bed and watched her hammering, I didn't say much either. When she'd gone I called to Timmy; our house had thin new walls, so a loud whisper reached him.

'Timmy?'

'What?' His voice was all hollow from crying.

'Why did you do it?'

'Do what?'

'You know. Why did you do it?'

'Don't know. It was an accident.'

'It didn't half look a mess,' I whispered, and I giggled, and then Timmy did, and then neither of us could stop, we laughed louder and louder until our mother came halfway up the stairs and told us to be quiet and go to sleep. It was a relief to stop laughing, my ribs ached and I felt so hot. We went on talking though: mum hadn't sounded angry yet.

'Hey. Timmy. Was it for your fort?'

'Yeah. I've got two hundred and forty now.'

'That's no good. You'll need thousands, you'll need millions I expect.'

Timmy was building the fort out of spent matches. He'd started off collecting them out of our father's ashtrays. He'd shown me the groundplan, two matches high, glued onto a piece of hardboard.

'That's why I was burning them. I thought it would be quicker.'

'What d'you touch the curtain for then?'

'I don't know. I just did.'

I liked the idea of the fort. It was to be a Wild West fort, of the kind we'd seen so often at the pictures or on television, rectangular with towers and stout wooden gates. You'd be safe inside a fort like that.

Timmy talked about the fort for a while. I could see it as clearly as he could, miniature and at the same time life-size, like my dollshouse. I talked about the dollshouse too, about how everything in it must work, be usable, the electric lights with tiny switches, the beds with real sheets, curtains you could pull closed in the evenings: so that someone could really use it, really live there.

Then Mum came a bit further up the stairs and yelled at us to shut up, so we did. Though I couldn't sleep at first. It was often hard to sleep, because of the noise, because of the television cursing and firing bullets up the stairs, or roaring applause as if there was a whole army packed into the front room, not just Mum and Dad sitting there quietly on their own. They were especially quiet when the TV was off. I could hardly hear a word they said, I used to imagine them whispering to each other, sitting on either end of the sofa, talking in quick whispers, arguing perhaps, fighting in hisses; more than once I had got out of bed and crouched on the landing trying to catch whether all was well or not but I hadn't been able to hear anything at all, not even a sigh.

That night, after Timmy's accident with my curtains, there must have been a drama on, there were lots of threatening voices and fierce little bits of music. I sang aloud to myself to block them out. Timmy sang a bit too. Then we went to sleep.

The next day was a Saturday. We got up late and after breakfast my mother gave me some money and told me to take Timmy to the pictures, she said she needed to get us out of her hair for once. I felt a little lick of uneasiness run all over me as she looked through her purse for the right money, because I could remember that she used to disapprove of going to Saturday matinees, saying that it was something children from the council estate did, that it was disgraceful to spend daylight hours in a dark stuffy cinema. I could remember her saying this, but not when, so there was no way of working out why she'd changed her mind. I didn't want to know anyway. I took the money, and Timmy's hand, and we went out.

The housing estate was still half building site in those days, a forbidden playground of breezeblocks and unexpected holes. The pavements were made but not the roads, the roads were rivers of yellowish rutted mud, lumpy with half-bricks, between the pavements. It was disconcerting to know that the road would one day be tarred or asphalted like a real road; it must mean that all roads hid simple earth beneath them, could perhaps be peeled away like elastoplast to show the earth still lying there underneath, all dank and flattened as earth looks when you lift aside a stone.

I used to worry about the worms as well. I couldn't walk along that riverbank pavement without thinking about the worms being tarmacked over and not able to burrow their way up and out.

'They'll burrow along underneath,' my mother had said.

'They'll come out on the other side, they'll be all right.'

But I was unconvinced, I couldn't see a worm having that much staying-power, I used to imagine exhaustion underground, and worms caught halfway over coming up against the tarmac and suffocating in the dark. So I walked along warning them all to get away before the tarmac came, I didn't attend to Timmy pulling at my hand or singing, I was directing my thoughts at the earthworms.

The cinema was a squat greyish building with THE REX in an arc of red neon over the door, left unlit for Saturday matinees. There was no queue, but a noisy playground crowd, someone hobbling about on roller skates, two girls sharing a skipping rope. As we crossed the road I saw Nicholas Bourne leaning up against the wall with two other boys; our eyes met but neither of us smiled.

Once I had met Nicholas Bourne by accident beside the marshes three fields beyond our house. He was with his friends. I didn't say much, but he had run up to me, his hands clasped in front of him.

'Look,' he'd said excitedly, 'look what I got,' and he'd opened his muddy hands to show me the grey soft baby moorhen he held.

I remember still the meek duckling curve of its head, its heartless-joke feet, enormous and pink as Brighton rock. It had bright empty eyes, eyes for just seeing things with.

'You can have him,' said Nicholas Bourne. 'You have him,' and he'd gently pushed the moorhen into my hands, and turned, and run off to join his friends calling through the copse past the marshes.

Well, how was I to know then that it was something I'd remember for the rest of my life? (That thrilling shock of delight, the warm down, the tender heartbeat against my fingers). Nicholas Bourne loves you, said the girl who sat next to me at school, but I had turned my head away, because he was stupid at reading aloud, and came from the council estate.

He blushed now, when he saw me in front of the cinema. Cheered by power, I dragged Timmy over to a friend of mine, the girl I sat next to in school, and told her about my bedroom curtains, and we clucked together over Timmy's head, and then she told lots of other people, and Timmy began to show off, as if he'd done it all on purpose, for thrills.

I was quite cross with him by the time the cinema doors opened, I told him he'd better behave or I'd leave him outside, and he settled down at once, as if he'd actually believed me. That made me think I'd really meant it too, I felt full of hatred for him standing there beside me with his ears sticking out and his hands in his pockets. I gave him a push out of this sudden hatred, and the lady at the door looked hard at me to let me know she'd seen.

I slunk past her and bought the tickets from the other lady in the kiosk. They were known to be sisters, the lady at the door and the lady in the kiosk, they both had little barrel bodies and long strong arms and white hair; I found it hard to believe that people so old could still be sisters, I felt that that was the sort of thing people usually grew out of.

I took Timmy down to the middle row, the girl I sat next to in class was saving us seats. Everyone was very noisy sitting there waiting for the cartoon to start, as if we wanted to underline that this was no schoolday or school outing, but a Saturday free-choice. There was also the feeling that here was a real grownup institution, a cinema, turned over to us, to children, which, while rather exciting, made the cinema itself altogether less formidable, rather like the effect Mr Fulljames had had one day on dinner duty, when he'd suddenly joined in with a game of leapfrog on the school meadow.

The whole point of the children's films, it seems to me now, was that we didn't have to watch them: that was what made them children's films. It was very different to going to the pictures in the evening with your parents, when the queue was grave and orderly, and people bought their tickets in a very subdued serious way, as if it was church they were going to.

On Saturdays you watched the film but talked loudly all the way through it, drowned out dialogue with your own sound-effects, whooped along with Tarzan as he swung from tree to tree, because you could if you wanted to.

Actually it was the boys that made most of the noise. The boys made the noise, the girls made no objection. That's how things were in those days.

I was to see, or half-see, quarter-hear, so many films on those Saturday mornings: Tarzan darkening lakes with clouds of black crocodile blood, Robin Hood in a gleaming pageboy, children outwitting hoodlums or saving tigers. But mainly it's cowboy

films I remember. There were dozens of Western series on the
television too at that time, and they and the Saturday morning
cowboys all merged and fitted together, mapping a second childhood landscape, that could in games be conjured up to fit over a
wet field in Kent: dry scrub, yellow grass, tumbleweeds blowing,
a distant shoulder of mountains, gesturing cacti, a hint of wild
Indians beyond the next rise.

Here and there was a face, too, that I remember still. I was in
love with one of the cowboys in Laramie on TV, and once to my
transfixed delight he turned up in a Saturday morning matinee,
using the wrong name but clearly still himself, moody, ill-
shaven, scornfully monosyllabic. It worried me occasionally that
there were so many cowboy films; I thought that if they kept on
being made at such a rate pretty soon everyone in the Wild West
would be completely accounted for, an uncomfortably claustro-
phobic notion. Besides, with fewer and fewer cowboys remaining private and anonymous, the odds were that sooner or later
their stories would start running into one another: delicious
Laramie Jess might stalk some day into a saloon and find himself
standing next to Texas John Slaughter, or Maverick, or
Cheyenne.

I saw them all sipping whiskey and staring uneasily into the
mirror that always backs Western saloon bars. Would each sense
the others' special resonance? Clearly they all were special: each
had an audience. They all carried on having adventures, being
shot at or knocked out and tied to wooden chairs, without
realizing that we were always watching them. Wouldn't our
unseen presence give them some strange aura, which might
make itself fully felt if they were all to come together and look
into one another's eyes? Might Laramie Jess notice Maverick's
hangers-on, even though he paid no attention to his own?

Though sometimes I had my suspicions about Laramie Jess:
sometimes he seemed aware of me. It was the way he used to
gallop about casually holding the reins with one hand. It never
failed to thrill me, but why was he bothering if he didn't think
someone was watching? He was showing off all right; everyone
else was sensible, everyone else held on with both hands.

Quite apart from the film and my enjoyable Western puzzling,
the Saturday matinee sometimes provided other more immediate
entertainments. More than once, while bullets flew or Tarzan

knuckled the latest crocodile, Saturday rowdiness spilled over, and fights broke out amongst the bad boys at the front, grey-flanelled bottoms up-ended as if in diving, and crushing noises as bodies rolled on the empty orange-drink cartons and discarded ice-cream cones on the floor.

Then the larger of the two cinema sisters, the one that stood guard by the door, would force her way through to the front and wordlessly wade out again, usually with a boy clutched by the scruff in either hand. We'd all go very quiet at this show of grownup, school-type authority, we'd all sit still while she dragged them up the aisle, their feet scrabbling at the carpet or bouncing hopelessly over the shallow steps; it was all rather thrilling.

The place would briefly flood with light as she kicked the doors open; and then Tarzan or the cowboys, still wrestling or galloping, would fade and dwindle like shadows when the sun goes in. You could see that they were only pictures, then: they'd look silly, outsized and silly, still carrying on up there on the screen while the cinema doors banged shut again and we all looked at one another instead of at them. We had been attending, or playing at attending, to Tarzan's drama, but he couldn't begin to attend to ours. He just kept swinging urgently through the trees whether we were watching him or not. It seemed a meek, belittled way to behave. I didn't really care when it happened to Tarzan, he looked so ridiculous anyway in his torn underwear and big naked arms; but I didn't like it happening to any of my entrancing cowboys. It was a bit like the way I treated Nicholas Bourne: you've got power over the people you don't listen to. I could see that, even then.

I never go to cinemas now. Haven't for years. It's a disability. I've tried as far as I can to make light of it, make it part of my personality, that a lover might use to take hold of me by, together with the long and ever-lengthening list of my allergies, those microscopic substances, or sometimes entire events, that start my body off in new attempts to kill me by not letting me breathe. This often takes place in some dramatic style, even now, involving bouts of cyanosis, ambulance sirens, oxygen masks and shots of adrenaline; nothing like it to pep up a relationship. Or so I've found.

Once he's called an ambulance for you a man often feels he's got the right to probe or judge. I let them make the usual connection: 'Yes, when I was eight. Just after my father – well, you know about my father. You know about him.'

He's part of my personality too, these days. How else can I account for him? I usually bring him in fairly early, to explain my various phobias and failures and physical shortcomings: it always works.

So the asthma started right after that, then? Mmm. That's interesting . . .

These men. They all say the same thing. They all started the same little fires. They all say the same thing.

What happened just after my father left is very blurred in my memory; partly, it's true, by illness. At first home felt better, there were fewer complicated silences at night. Once I saw my mother drop a jug in the kitchen. It slipped out of her hand as she was drying it, and when it hit the floor and smashed she stood staring down at it for a few seconds and then burst out crying. She held the tea-towel over her eyes. There was a map of Yorkshire printed on the tea-towel, I can still see Richmond Castle if I close my eyes.

Still she spoke comfortable words to me: Daddy was away on business, staying away for a little holiday, visiting Grandma, sending his love, looking forward to seeing us all soon. I was a child, it was my part to believe her. I swallowed her lies, but it felt like swallowing stones.

And at last the girl who sat next to me in school turned towards me, her voice all sympathy, her eyes alive.

'Here, zit true, your dad's gone off?'

My mother should have realized that would happen.

'They gonna get divorced?'

Well, yes, eventually, I suppose they did. They must've done. I never asked about it, not even when I was growing up, and curious. Why did he leave like that? Was it another woman? Didn't he ever want to see me? Did he ever try to see me, and did you stop him? I never asked, for fear of what my mother might try to make me believe.

He wrote to me once, when I was about seventeen. I didn't

write back, though he gave an address. He seemed an
irrelevance by then. I had my own problems, he was nothing to
do with me.

Except.

Indirectly.

Yes. Here: the fossilized secret at the heart of me. I've kept it
there so long.

Here. This is what happened.

Sometimes Timmy and I slept together in those days just after
my father left. I'd wake up and find him standing by my bed,
looking at me in the half-light from the landing, left on all night
now. He'd climb in and we'd lie back-to-back, not speaking, not
touching. My mother didn't like it though, I don't know why.
Once she dragged Timmy out in the morning and smacked him,
and even I could see she felt guilty about it, about hitting him.

I think it was that evening, or an evening soon afterwards, that
she took us to the pictures. I think she was wanting us to feel that
things were getting back to normal. It was a summer evening,
still and beautiful. The houses were nearly all finished by then,
people were beginning to move in at places that had been muddy
holes in the ground the previous winter.

'More children for you to play with,' said my mother as we
trooped past the newly tarmacked road, 'more *nice* children.'

Serves them right, I thought, back with the earthworms.
Stupid things. Serves them right. Nicholas Bourne had written
me a love-letter. I had glanced at it and torn it up in front of him.
Everyone was being very nice to me at school. Nearly everyone.
No one objected if I stared out of the window during history or
burst into tears and ran away into the cloakroom. I used to cry a
lot in maths lessons, and spent most of them daydreaming in the
girls' toilet. No one told me off, not yet.

We walked towards the village. Another field on the way had
just been sold to developers.

'It's a shame,' said my mother. 'In a way,' she added.

'It was apples, where you live,' Nicholas Bourne had said to
me, 'and damsons.'

The Rex in the evening: neon-lit, grave adults queueing,
children's hands held. My mother held mine. In my other hand,

safe in my blazer pocket – a box of matches, rough one side like a nailfile, scented with carbon. They were a comfort to me, better than Timmy's fort or the dollshouse my father would never build for me. I had carried the matches for about a week, by then. The box was growing rounded with fondling.

My mother bought us choc-ices. I can remember some scenes from the film, which was a comedy: a donkey wearing a straw hat, a team of men diving off a high rock in unison. I liked the film and laughed a lot.

We walked home in the twilight. It seemed a long way home. I felt so heavy I could hardly lift my feet up. The box of matches made my arm ache all the way up to my shoulder.

I had gone to the Rex's toilet after the film had ended. It was a chilly place even in summer, with pale green walls, a wooden seat, and red velvet curtains matching those inside the cinema. When I'd pulled the chain I took the matchbox out and tapped it open. I took a match out: round red head, clean stripped little body.

I struck it. I saw the tender flame. I thought first about the curtains, because of what Timmy had done to mine, so long ago it seemed by then. I imagined the little flame coasting about in all that softness. I thought of the way the cloth would change, with firing: new scalloped edges, a charcoal fragility. I blew the match out, dropped it, lit another. I was not playing with matches. I was not playing.

It was the translation that I wanted to concentrate on; I could feel its power while a match was burning. Translation: tender little flame into roaring furnace. And everything could burn. Everything would burn: all real things, lampshades and carpets, tables and armchairs, all those solid things. They'd all burn, they'd all just sit there, burning.

With matches I could turn one thing into another thing. I could make the hearthrug turn into the fire, I could make the curtains come alive and writhe upon the walls, I could use transforming magic on the solid grownup world.

I lit the second match, and I laid it, still burning, in the wastepaper bin, a metal thing half-full of screwed-up sweetpapers, an empty toilet-roll, a discarded blue hair-ribbon, with one dark hair still caught in the knot. I could see it would all burn well.

I closed the door gently behind me. The cinema was empty and closing for the night, there was only one show during the week. We walked home in the twilight. It seemed a long way.

The cinema burnt to the ground. So did the bungalow next door, where the two sisters lived. One of them, the strong-armed fight-breaker, was overcome by smoke in her bedroom, and died of suffocation before the ambulance arrived.

Of course it was an accident. I hadn't meant anyone to die. But then I don't quite know what I meant. I didn't kill her on purpose. It was an accident.

No one ever connected it all with me. I was in hospital a lot myself at the time, with my lungs turning themselves on and off. I screamed in my sleep a good deal, but who wouldn't, losing health and father all at once?

I missed so much schooling that I had to stay down a year, and knew no one in my class when I finally went back to school. I couldn't walk far without wheezing and the steroids I was on made me a funny shape, round-faced, hefty. No more letters or love-tokens from Nicholas Bourne. I didn't mind very much, it felt safer being someone else.

The cinema was never rebuilt. They were going out of fashion anyway, I suppose. I remember looking at the blackened rubble and realizing that never again would I sit there and watch Laramie Jess narrow his soft brown eyes in the sunshine or gallop one-handed across those dry familiar plains. That was my land of lost content. And I destroyed it all by myself.

It's easy to imagine that it was the fire, the murder, that have made me what I am. I told no one. I remembered the story of Midas's ears, and how the reeds spread the rumour: I didn't even tell the ground my secret. I kept it inside me until it fossilized like a sharp piece of ancient bone. Some men have found it beguiling for a while, that secret part, until they begin to see it as something tedious and deformed, because I cannot let anyone get too close, tell anyone any version of the truth.

Though I hardly know for certain what the truth is, or why the truth was. I can sum up: the matchbox was disaster, I Pandora. I wanted power, I opened the box, struck the engulfing flame; years later I'm still clawing at my eyes.

Or there again, perhaps not: it's consoling to make these

dramatic patterns. But really it just won't do, to make too much sense of the past. No.

Still, I like to hear other people's stories, little comical arson stories, the sort I would have been able to cap, perhaps, if no one had died.

Oh yeah? Grandmother's bed, eh? Then listen, when I was eight years old I set the local cinema on fire –

No. Hardly. Not when someone died.

I wish it had been me though, Red Riding Hood with matches, burning my grandmother's bed. I wish it had been me, sparking off a squadron of fragile paper aeroplanes, watching them spiralling down in harmless flames.

I wish that had been me.

That's all.

SISTER
HILARY

SISTER HILARY was due to retire, or I might not have taken the job. It was only for a few months in any case, until my midwifery course started. Still, I was apprehensive. I'd worked on her ward as a student. She was the sort of sister I've heard elderly consultants reminisce about.

'You never saw a bed-sore, you could tell the time on her ward by which side the patients were lying on. Turned two-hourly on the dot, that's how it was done –'

Two elderly consultants, to be precise. Perhaps they were remembering the same woman. I must say I was rather taken with this notion the first time I heard about it, picturing an entire Nightingale wardful of hapless pyjama'd patients all being ruthlessly turned like rows of mattresses, never getting to see one another's faces, addressing, perhaps, occasional furtive conversational whispers to the backs of one another's ears.

Though how, as I said to my flatmate afterwards, you were supposed to tell the time by it beat me. She suggested that, given at least twenty-four patients, it might be possible to work out some fairly simple posturing-system so that anyone in on the code would be able to calculate the time perfectly well, though as time-keeping devices went it would certainly be a cumbersome one, if more reliable than sundials in bad weather.

Actually by the time I arrived on Hilary ward we were all meant to be throwing out the old patients-as-clockwork idea and going in for something called the Nursing Process. At the end of my first week on the ward all we students had to go to a lecture about it, given by a rather fat American doctoral research student wearing a kaftan and big sticky-looking wooden beads.

'The Nursing Process,' she explained, 'is the practical application of the concept of patient individuality.' She wasn't that easy to follow but the basic idea, as far as I could make it out, was that patients, being individuals, deserved individualized care: each nurse should be assigned a particular bunch of patients, learn all about them – the Nursing Process admission form the research student passed around bristled with intimate questions – and carry out all necessary nursing care for them, reports to be written at shift's end not, as now, by the sister in charge, but by the nurse, even the student nurse, who had actually looked after the patient concerned.

The old ways ('You do the baths, I'll do the dressings') were task-orientated, the research student pointed out; the new way was *patient*-orientated. I was busily writing all this down when I noticed the research student's shoes, and stopped listening. They were black, with small square heels, splayed with age and her weight I suppose, and cut very low in the front, displaying the plump beginnings of all her toes like two rows of little cleavages.

I'd quickly developed an obsession with breasts, working on Hilary ward. That very morning I'd been doing a quiet chatty locker-round when a pretty blonde patient in her thirties, who for religious reasons had refused all operative treatment, had insisted on showing me the cause of the trouble; she'd unbuttoned her nightdress with what seemed like pride:

'See, look!' displaying one normal breast, meek and drooping the same as anyone else's, and one immense and stiffly perfect globe, creamily dirigible as a *Playboy* centrefold's, a male fantasy breast.

'It's rock-hard,' said the patient, 'touch it, go on.'

And since I couldn't instantly think of a reason not to, at least not a kind one, I reached my unwilling fingers out and touched that dreadful perfection, warm marble, a statue's breast.

'Full of cancer,' said the patient, at once calm and eager, 'I 'spect it's in the other one by now.'

I told the Hilary ward Staff Nurse about all this while we did the drug round, and she was horrified and amused, and repeated the story to the afternoon shift at hand-over. I happened to pass the office at the right time, I heard the blonde woman's name mentioned and hung about outside, listening.

'... Frightened the poor little student half to death,' finished the Staff Nurse, over the mixed enjoyable gasps of laughter and disgust, 'honestly, what a nutter – '

I went on with the afternoon temperatures, elated, since I'd evidently experienced something worth talking about, and slightly nettled at the same time; I hadn't been frightened so much as nonplussed, placed in an entirely unprecedented situation; and I'm not little, I was taller than the Staff Nurse.

Still nonplussed I went on staring at the doctoral research student's matching sets of reminiscent toes until I remembered to listen to her as well.

'I shall be visiting with every clinical area in turn,' she was saying, 'to discuss implementation of the Nursing Process in each ward-situation.'

I couldn't help smiling to myself at that. Sister Hilary would make mincemeat of her and her gentle earnest talk of patient individuality. Sister Hilary went in for bath books, turn books, dressing books and discipline. I tried to imagine the research student bearding Sister Hilary in the den of her own ward-situation, hers alone for, it was said, more than twenty-five years.

I couldn't see much discussion going on, at any rate not the sort the research student was envisaging. You didn't really discuss anything with Sister Hilary, you just apologized and got out of range as fast as possible.

'I hope you can run in those shoes,' I thought at the research student, with some of that schoolroom glee you feel when the teacher's toying with somebody else.

'Though implementation will be carried out piecemeal, over a period of one to two years.'

And over Sister Hilary's dead body, I jokily told my flatmate that evening, but she said that she thought ward sisters deserved autonomy, that if it was taken away now from the old guard, we'd have none ourselves, when it was time for us to succeed them. We ended up having quite an argument about it.

'I mean, it's not you on bloody Hilary ward,' I told her.

'Well, God, I might as well be – '

It was true, I did go on about Sister Hilary. She was so shamelessly power-loving and selfish in the way men often are, the ones who can sit about reading the paper while you do the washing-up.

She was a small round-shouldered woman with a pink pouched face, often slitty-eyed with rage. She was the only sister I ever saw who never wore an apron, never once lent a hand with the beds. Often, hearing her telephone ring, I'd have to drop what I was doing — a blanket-bath, a dressing — and pound down the ward along the corridor to her office, where she'd be sitting motionless, glowering at the time I'd taken to get there, the telephone shrilling on the desk beside her hand.

'She just feels it's not her job to answer it,' the Staff Nurse explained. 'She says it's the ward clerk's job.'

'But we haven't got a ward clerk.'

'No, but we ought to have one. It's a protest, if you like. I mean, you can see she's got a point.'

'Oh yeah ...' I was scornful. 'Why can't we write anything down in report then, what's the point of that?'

'Well, it's supposed to be good for your memory, you know, that's how she used to do it – '

'Come on, they had a much slower patient turnover then, people were in bed for weeks, they're just in and out now, it's impossible to remember everything, you know it is.'

'Look,' said the Staff Nurse, giving up, 'don't ask me, I just work here. You can nip into the office while she's at lunch and write it all down if you have to, but don't say I told you to and don't get caught – '

But of course Sister kept on catching us, all the time, suddenly emerging from her office for a quick prowl round just as you were chatting to a patient, or furtively noting something down on the back of your apron (well-starched aprons are handy for this) and once she came upon me in the private room, giving a patient a blanket-bath using the sink beside the bed.

'Just what do you think you are doing, nurse!'

Muscles bounced and fluttered in her throat; still clutching my soapy dripping facecloth, I stammered with reflex guilt, 'Oh, I – '

'Why aren't you using a bowl? Clear the locker top at once please, and use the correct equipment, I will not have my nurses take it upon themselves to ignore their basic training. Kindly carry out procedures as you were taught to, nurse!' Her emphasis on the last word was alike definition and contempt. She'd raged very loudly, everyone on the lower end of the ward must have heard her. I remember I felt almost ill with embarrassment, my fingers pricked with the pins-and-needles of shock. And the patient in the private room was a shy elderly lady; I felt her eyes on me as the door banged shut, and knew that she was frightened, not only by Sister's rage, but also by me, because I'd provoked it: been proven incompetent, and she still in my hands.

It didn't always work like that. Once Sister Hilary had a high old time with the other student there, who was even more junior than I was and who'd realized, just as she pulled the chain, that she'd thrown out a specimen from someone on a twenty-four hour urine collection.

Sister had been deeply shocked and grieved; had pointed out at length the inconvenience of beginning the collection again, the increased delay in diagnosis this involved, and the quite possibly serious repercussions of such a delay on the life and health of the patient concerned. She ended (this was during report) with a general lecture on the scarcely credible levels of inefficiency and dolt-like stupidity invariably displayed by us all, and then let us loose on the ward. The other student shot off at once for a quick traditional cry in the sluice-room, but it wasn't enough, she went on sobbing at intervals while we made the beds, no matter what I said to her.

'Honest, Sylvia, everyone does it, I've done it, and that was when I could write everything down, it wasn't your fault. Anyway, I bet it doesn't really matter – '

But she stayed white and quiet until the patient whose bed we'd just reached, a big bold-eyed woman only in for her piles, smiled at Sylvia from her chair and said, 'S'that old bag, isn't it? Shall I black her eye for you?' and we all laughed, all the patients within hearing joined in and it was as if a door had opened:

'God, she scares the living daylights out of me – '

'Didn't know they still made them like that – '

'I just try to keep out of her way – '

'Oh I had a visitor on Tuesday dear, my cousin Eric, he's a sick man himself, he was coming all the way from Billericay, and the train was late, and she wouldn't let him in, lovey, not for five minutes, all the way from Billericay, you won't let her near me after my op, will you, lovey?'

(This last from a very old lady, whose face I still remember, who on the whole liked being in hospital, I knew, because she was so lonely at home; whom we juniors all furtively kissed goodbye as she was wheeled away to the operating theatre, and who died two days afterwards in ITU, never having woken up again.)

'. . . You won't let her near me after my op, will you lovey?'

I was entirely surprised by that sudden chorus, though I didn't quite notice this at the time. It seems to me now that what surprised me most was not so much that the patients spoke out, but that they had noticed in the first place; remembered the rages, felt the atmosphere, and taken sides. I had somehow assumed that anyone being looked after is going to stop looking back; so I was almost as surprised as if a newsreader, or someone on Coronation Street, had suddenly leaned out through the screen into my living-room and told me how much they liked my new curtains.

The truth is that part of the fun of being a nurse, or a doctor, is that your patients, their courage or terrors, their relations, their strange preferences and secret habits – their lives, in short – are on show to you; they come, exist, and go, like a TV soap opera; or like foreign countries we can tour through and reminisce about when we're safely back home. And you at least start off with the feeling that you'll learn something just from seeing it all, an illusion common to travellers.

Listen: one of the reasons I embarked on midwifery was my reaction to a scene I witnessed on the obstetric ward I was sent to after my spell on Hilary.

A woman whose baby had died was in labour, and ready to deliver. Her husband and the midwife were taking her, in her bed, across the corridor to the delivery room, when the married pair started a sort of wretched argument.

'Please, look, you said you wanted me to – '

'No, I'll be all right, no, you stay here – '

I went and told Sister what was happening. The Sister on the obstetric ward was a nice young woman, with pink cheeks and smooth efficient hair.

'Right, go and make some more tea,' she told me, and went off briskly to collect the husband, now standing dazedly alone outside the closed delivery-room doors. I passed them as I went to the kitchen. She was talking to him softly, taking his arm to walk him back to her quiet office. Her eyes met mine very briefly as I passed, and I felt her excitement, her anxious pleasure: she was comforting him.

I felt that excitement too, we all did, a whole shiftful of nurses longing to console. It was such a pure tragedy, and well-precedented; we all wanted to do our bit, by the husband, by the wife, we all wanted a go, you could almost feel it in the air.

Though it was still entirely genuine sympathy, and it helped. When I took the teatray into Sister's office the man was already a better colour, he was able to look up when I entered, even to say thank you. Whatever Sister had said or done had been the right things, her comforting had been no less effective because she had enjoyed giving it. Was her altruism less valid, because she had enjoyed feeling it?

I didn't think so, still don't. But I can't help feeling, now, that her response, and the shift's, was essentially a theatrical one: a response to drama. Suppose you could reach in, at the play's end, not just sit there crying in the stalls, but reach in with your practised comforting talk, hot tea, real sympathy? You're still part of the audience, mind, it's not *your* problem you're crying about, it's theirs.

For me as a student that scene on the obstetrics ward summed up all nursing's thrilling appeal – a dangerous one, I'm inclined to think now. The whole incident, its complex dramas, stayed photographically vivid in my memory, presenting itself to me now and then to be pondered over, seeming to hint at some special truth. The things you see in hospitals often do, but perhaps this is particularly true of maternity wards. I expect quite a few have taken up midwifery or obstetrics with some vague notion that familiarity with the various joyous or catastrophic results of sex would somehow shed light on the wider mysteries of life in general. I'd learn, and yet I would be safe: inside a clean white gown and sterile gloves. And I'd be in charge.

Rich roles, in nursing or medicine: saviour, boss, comforter, sightseer; tourist in the foreign places of other people's lives.

My memory still presents me with snapshots, mementoes of my earlier days, my nurse's Grand Tour. I can turn to them now, when they're furry with age, and see after all that my own faded youthful image is there, too, in every one.

Of course I had my doubts about staffing for Sister Hilary. But it was only for a few months, and she was due to retire, and said besides to have lost some of her old fire after suffering a mild and private stroke the year before. I decided that I'd be able to put up with her perfectly easily; she was, I remarked to my (by then ex-) flatmate on the way to our weekly yoga class, merely that sort of bully who needs to be stood up to. I spoke sneeringly, I considered this a pretty distasteful sort of thing to need; all the same the thought of doing all the standing-up made me feel quite pleasantly aggressive and assured.

But I'd got Sister Hilary all wrong. She wasn't that sort of bully at all.

The stroke hadn't altered her. I'd half expected a limp or a drawn lop-sided face, and been a little frightened at the prospect of pretending not to notice; but she looked exactly the same as she had three years earlier, same neat figure, hunched but alert, same pink face. The only difference was that the face now smiled at me.

'Ah, hallo, welcome!' and she shook my hand. She gave no sign of recognizing me, but then she'd no doubt seen a good few new faces since mine had passed by. She showed me round the ward, which hadn't changed either. We walked past the bed where the blonde woman had shown me the worst, and I wondered again what had happened to her, or rather, how long it had taken to happen.

'I do so hope you will enjoy working here – '

We passed a student, who kept her back turned; I remembered doing that too, pretending to be unaware that Sister was on the prowl; like keeping your head down when the teacher's glaring.

'I'll give you a report over coffee, I think . . .'

Back in her office I saw that she was still using the old kardex, not the expansive Nursing Process one.

'Do read through it for yourself if you like. Do you take sugar?'

'Ah, no thank you – '

While she was pouring out I opened the kardex on my lap. It made me feel helpless.

'I ah need to make a few notes,' I said, trying to sound as non-aggressive and unassured as possible. 'I hope you don't mind?'

'Not at all,' said this new Sister Hilary.

I was unsurprised at this by now; I was beginning to get some glimpse of the world through her eyes. I could make most sense of it by seeing her as a lady of the old type, an Edwardian, constantly amazed and infuriated by the clumsiness of those untaught domestics, her students. Qualification had made me her social equal, junior of course but still her guest. And if I spilt the milk or blew on my tea she'd politely allow me to, the gracious hostess pretending not to notice social ineptitude. I'd get away with it; though the kitchen maid who dropped a tea-tray was still fair game. I thought of the student carefully keeping her back turned; tears were still being shed in the sluice-room, it seemed.

I thought all this while I was looking at the kardex, feeling helpless. I could scarcely read it. The night-nurse's bits were clear enough, and the occasional late Staff Nurse's contributions. But most of it was Sister Hilary's, and she could hardly write. The stroke had cut a few essential wires after all, leaving her with something that looked like writing at a distance, but close to more like scribbles a baby might make, playing at joined-up writing. Occasional flattened angularities showed that she had laid a ruler along the lines, to try to keep them level. I could make out the odd word. You can see why I wanted to sound unchallenging.

'I ah need to make a few notes, I hope you don't mind?'

'Not at all.'

I gathered most of what I needed from the legible bits, and then we talked about linen supplies, which are the nursing equivalent of the weather, always unpredictable and usually cause for complaint.

'She's not that sort of bully at all,' I told my ex-flatmate a few days later, and I explained about the Edwardian-lady idea.

But she said it sounded more like a public-school type cruelty, that I wasn't a transformed servant so much as a grown-up fag.

'I bet she remembers you as well, she just pretends she doesn't. Like cabinet ministers and so on, I bet they don't say, Oh yeah I remember you, you were my fag at Eton, I bet nobody says anything, not when they're all grown-up, but they all know, all the same, they all remember.'

'Oh, well, I don't think it matters much. She's retiring soon anyway.'

'Good thing too.'

I gave her a look, and she said that she thought it was patronizing to be sorry for people merely because they'd grown old.

But I wasn't just sorry for Sister Hilary. She had made me suffer once, I couldn't help having other more complicated emotions about her as well. I was slightly anxious with her, afraid that she would forget the rules and bark at me again; often I heard myself fawning at her, admiring her new handbag, carefully watering the plants in her office. Asked, I would have said that I disliked her, that she was really rather a monster in her way, a small-time autocrat; yet I went on treating her with a sort of craven affection. I wanted to please her. And I watched her: she was a real puzzle.

Because I was her equal, the transformed servant, the grown-up fag, Sister Hilary talked to me, she told me stories. She used to take me to early lunch and tell me the sort of stories nurses always have a store of: diagnoses missed; massive overdoses accidentally given (but generally survived); the old lady admitted to the ward via Casualty where, volubly anxious about wasting the doctor's time, she'd complained of a tight wedding-ring and resultant soreness, and whose glove was peeled off to reveal a finger perfectly black with gangrene; and (told teasingly), the tale of the ghostly nurse on the children's ward, the wretched spirit of a night-nurse who'd fallen asleep with a baby in her lap, and suffocated it, appearing now to lay her chilly warning hand on the shoulder of anyone nodding over a late-night feed.

'Um, when did you, I mean, were you nursing during the war?'

'Ah, the war ...'

Sister Hilary remembered buzz-bombs, had flung herself under the nearest bed when the engines stopped, whilst fierce upright ward sisters paused in their labours only long enough to brush the plaster and brickdust from their aprons, and re-tie their frilly caps.

I was entranced by that one, not only by the ramrod old sisters but by the picture of my Sister Hilary diving under a bed like a frightened pussycat; being young enough to move so fast. She'd been a new staff nurse then, a newly grown-up fag herself. When had she started to abuse and humiliate her students? I remembered still that strange patient chorus, She scares the living daylights out of me, Don't let her near me after my op, will you, lovey?

When had she started to bully her patients? And why? That was the puzzle. I watched her for clues.

I thought at first that a major clue lay in the way she treated the doctors, especially during ward rounds, which on Hilary ward had a great deal of the ritualized solemnity generally associated with royal visits: Mr Craddock the King-Emperor, Sister his colonial viceroy, honoured by his presence, confident of his complete approval. She treated all three consultants like that but Mr Craddock, who must have been close to retirement himself, seemed to be Senior Crowned Head. Besides he was more inclined to hang about afterwards accepting cups of tea.

I used to look at him nibbling on a Digestive and remember dashing round the ward as a student cramming all the patients' private belongings into their lockers so that Mr Craddock would not be offended by sticky squash bottles or bowls of sweets; I remembered crouching down to floor level to eye up all the bed-wheels, which must be placed exactly in alignment like soldiers drawn up for review.

They had annoyed me a great deal at the time, these minute preparations, not only because they were time-wasting but also because they seemed to me to be just the sort of details that a man would never notice anyway, which made them even more of a humiliation. They weren't something anyone had ever asked for; I was sure Mr Craddock didn't go around demanding beds-at-attention, it was something Sister Hilary had made up, a bed-straightening ritual, in his honour. How many years had he walked through the ward never noticing this constantly offered and useless gift? But perhaps he would have noticed if we'd stopped doing it; perhaps he would have sensed a lessening of something like love?

Still if he didn't notice the detail I'm sure he felt the general glow; he seemed to enjoy that twice-weekly quadrille.

'More tea, Mr Craddock?'

'Ah, thank you Sister, excellent brew – '

And we would all chat about the patients, or Mr Craddock and Sister would go on and on about people they knew who had retired. In which case the rest of us would get a bit restless, we all had work to do; once or twice the junior houseman caught my eye and flashed me a youth-freemasonry message of such frantic boredom that I had to look away quickly so that I didn't laugh out loud.

Even so, Sister Hilary treated all these medical men with polite reverence, varying its degree slightly according to each man's seniority. The registrars almost got the full-blown consultant-treatment, the junior houseman something altogether less formal, though Sister still rose to her feet whenever he dropped in to the office, and laughed, in a series of dry little coughs, at all his mild attempts at humour. He was rather a nice-looking young man, and he flirted with her.

'Oh, good morning doctor, do come in and have a little chat – '

'Sister Hilary, how can I keep away?'

I was in the office myself during this exchange, on the telephone to the laundry, and while Sister's back was turned he looked over at me and winked. I couldn't help smiling back but still I felt a bit chilled. Sister Hilary had been running a ward for more years than he had been alive: yet he was her senior, professionally, already, in charge of her, responsible for her actions, which I thought gave all that faintly coy teasing a certain edge.

It struck me then that the doctors who gave me orders would not always be older than I was, but would inevitably get younger and younger, like policemen were supposed to. I was accustomed to obeying my elders, it feels natural to. But what when your seniors seemed like children to you, how would that feel? Perhaps you wouldn't know how to cope with it at all, perhaps you'd go overboard trying to convince yourself that you didn't in the least mind being ordered about by super-qualified children.

Nursing was like the army, I thought; we were all stuck as privates, no chance of a commission. RSM was the most you could hope for. Weren't RSMs traditionally brutal to their newest underling recruits, permanently enraged by years of saluting a constant parade of fresh-faced Sandhurst graduates?

And the doctors were all men, too, in those days. No doubt Sister Hilary had been brought up to defer to men, and did so as naturally as I did to my elders. But I didn't always defer with inward grace of course. Was it an added irritant, one no real RSM would have had to put up with, to be ordered about by members of the opposite sex?

Even if it wasn't, even if it was after all more of a comfort, a constant underlining of the traditional status quo, I still thought I could see some reason now behind all that ritualized gift-offering, the frantic polishing and locker-clearing and bed-straightening: it was an attempt not so much to honour the men as to justify a lifetime's subordination: if the idol wasn't on quite a tall enough pedestal, you could make it seem higher by the simple act of kneeling down.

I passed the RSM theory on to my ex-flatmate, who looked

bored and said that all I ever did was go on about things being like other things, and that this wouldn't get me anywhere at all.

'Honestly, suppose she's not like an Edwardian lady or a public schoolboy or a sergeant major, suppose she's just like a nurse, because that's what *nurses* are like?'

I said that the real point was that all nurses weren't like her, that she was like herself, that I wanted to know what she'd started off like, and that most conversation consisted of comparing certain things to other things, but all my ex-flatmate really wanted to know was which junior houseman I'd been talking about.

'Oh, him, is it. He's going out with Celia Shaw, you know, the one on Purdey ward with ginger hair.'

'Is he?'

'Mm. I worked with him once, on Mortimer, didn't think that much of him.'

'No?'

'Not too bright if you ask me.'

I shrugged my shoulders, but I was thinking, So! From her tone I was almost certain that she had looked at him, that he'd failed to look back, and that there was now a faint new rivalry between us, unspoken, as always. I changed the subject, but I was still thinking about the junior houseman. Somehow he seemed much more interesting than he had before.

The retirement party wasn't really my affair, I was too new. My opposite number, the senior Hilary ward Staff Nurse, who'd advised me not to get caught checking the kardex when I was a student, did most of the organizing. She would be Sister Hilary herself soon. She came round one afternoon when Sister was off duty. She was a bit self-conscious and giggly, being, as she put it, in mufti on her own ward. She had an envelope for contributions and, already, a big pastel Happy Retirement card for everyone to sign.

'What are you going to get her?' I asked.

'God knows. Got any ideas?'

'Well —'

'I mean, I don't know what she does with herself when she's not here. I can't imagine, to be honest.'

'Pottery,' I said. 'She does pottery. She goes to evening classes.'

'Really? Does she? How do you know?'

'She told me.'

The other Staff Nurse laughed. 'Really, I can't imagine it somehow. She really tell you that?'

'Mm.'

'Oh. Oh well.' I could see she was a bit put out; she'd been trying to please Sister Hilary far longer than I had.

'Well right then, pottery, have to see what I can do, thanks very much ...' and she went away a good deal less giggly than she'd been when she'd arrived. I felt rather disturbed too. I'd been giving report before she came so an office-full of students had heard our exchange. I could see that I'd given them something of a weapon, that evening classes in pottery would strike them as pretty pathetic, complete proof of loneliness. I didn't think that this was altogether a bad thing, Sister was still, even in these last weeks, as unkindly demoralizing to her clumsy young recruits as ever; still I was a little ashamed of myself, as if I'd got one over on the senior Staff Nurse by betraying a confidence. Perhaps I had. I thought the pottery was rather pathetic myself. Besides, the episode that had prompted Sister Hilary to tell me about it in the first place still makes me squirm a little when I think of it.

I'd stopped being afraid of her. I'd begun to answer her stories with ones of my own; I'd begun to tease her. Once Mr Craddock had been in a real hurry, whisked himself and his team round the ward and out again with barely time to say hallo, let alone notice all the kow-towing.

'Oh, I have such a headache,' she said to me later that morning.

'Do you want some aspirin?'

'Oh,' she sighed dramatically, 'and what good would that do me?'

I pretended to consider, then said, in tones of kindly encouragement, 'Well ... it'd make your stomach bleed – '

She looked hard at me for a moment, meeting my grin, then laughed her dry coughing laugh, and I could see she was thinking that there was more to me than she had at first supposed, which was what I had wanted her to think.

It was suddenly easy to make her laugh, so I went on doing it. Her behaviour towards me changed, gradually became rather like the way she behaved to the junior houseman, almost coy. Teasing was tact, with her. I was even able to use it, once or twice, to get my own way. I poked fun at her handwriting, told her it made me feel seasick and boss-eyed; which reassured her, I suppose, that I thought it a quirk of individuality, not a badge of sick old age. Anyway she laughed, and let me write the kardex myself from then on, which saved everyone a lot of time at report.

One day at lunch I told her the story of the mad old lady admitted to a psychiatric hospital, having implored her doctor for days past to do something about the glittering eyes in the ceiling, that kept staring down at her all the time; and how a social worker, visiting the flat to fill a suitcase for her, had popped into the living-room and found the ceiling drilled full of spy-holes by the equally mad people living in the flat upstairs.

Sister Hilary liked that one.

'I shall have to be careful,' she said, 'I live in a flat myself.' I saw her getting home in the early evening, putting her hard square handbag down on a chair, everything very neat, china like my grandmother's stacked in a cabinet, and a pendulum clock ticking on the wall, not quite drowned by the sound of someone else's music, Radio One perhaps, from the flat next door.

'You must come for a visit,' said Sister Hilary, breaking in on all this. 'Perhaps you're free for a cup of tea this afternoon?'

I was completely taken aback, and horribly embarrassed, imagining her claiming me as some sort of daughter-figure, of being trapped into a real relationship. Panic must have showed in my eyes, I was too surprised to hide it, though I was able to refuse the invitation on the perfectly truthful grounds that I had to be home early to get to my yoga class.

'I do evening classes myself,' she'd said quite smoothly in reply. 'In pottery. I shall be able to devote more time to it, when I retire.'

I told my ex-flatmate all about this while we were having a drink after class that night.

'It's funny,' I said, 'I almost like her in a way. She's so awful, she's so definite. Most people, you can't pin them down, they're not one thing or the other. I can't help liking her, she's just so completely awful.'

'Shame about the patients.'

There was something slightly hostile in this piety; she was in a bad mood despite all the yoga, she was working up to something.

'She doesn't have much to do with them these days,' I said, 'she's marking time.'

'What, two weeks more to go?'

'Mm.'

Pause.

'We'll get the Nursing Process once she's gone,' I said.

'Oh, that . . . I must say I rather admire her, keeping it all at bay so long.'

'Oh? What d'you mean?'

'Well, I think she's right. Basically. I reckon it's a waste of time.'

'What? The Nursing Process?'

'Yes. Just a lot more paperwork, as far as I can see. Asking all those daft questions, what's the point?'

'Well, you know. It helps you know them better, helps you plan their care properly. And they get to know you better.'

'Who says that's such a good thing?'

'How can it be bad?'

'I don't know, I just don't necessarily trust the thinking behind it all. They're trying to regulate kindness – why should that work any better than the old way? What really matters is whether you're Sister Hilary, or whether you're not, right?'

'I suppose –'

'You can't give an institution a caring face, so why bother to pretend about it? And it's no good thinking that for the patients to get to know us will help, it won't. We're not that important. To them. Not really. We're bit-parts. It's like, we're kidding ourselves. We hardly really matter at all, or only at the time. You've seen all those adverts, all those dopey posters, People Remember Nurses, well, I don't think they do remember us, it's us that remembers them. Isn't it?'

'No, I think it works both ways. Not that I've thought about it much.'

'No, you're too busy chasing after Whatsisface.'

Aha, I thought, cottoning on at last. I looked over at her and remembered that I'd never liked any of her boyfriends much, whereas she'd often liked mine, even gone out with one of my exes for a while. I liked her being jealous, it made me feel safer. I smiled at her; she knew she'd given herself away, and presently we laughed at one another.

'Tricky landing him, is it?'

'Oh, I think I'll manage.'

'Stopped seeing Celia then?'

'So he says.'

'So she says.'

'Well, thank *you*,' I said.

The retirement party was held in a small sitting-room in one of the nurses' homes, a new tower-block ten minutes walk from the old hospital. There was sherry or orange squash, and plates of little sausages and triangular sandwiches; this was before the days of quiche.

I'd half expected Sister Hilary to look older out of uniform; what really surprised me was how small she was. The starched cap had added about three inches, without it she scarcely came up to my shoulder. Her dark green suede shoes looked very new, the way old ladies' shoes often look, because they don't get walked about in very much.

The Director of the Nursing School made a speech about high standards and a lifetime lived for others, and various other similiar faces said much the same thing, and we all clapped, a little light smattering sound, while Sister Hilary (who'd been referred to throughout as Miss Green, which confused me at first) stepped up smartly enough to take her gift-wrapped box, which turned out to contain an enormous cut glass bowl and a big shiny book, with lots of photographs, called *Pottery Through the Ages*. She just smiled and nodded over the applause, she didn't make a speech.

'Where's your master, then?' I asked Stephen, who was clapping next to me.

He shook his head. 'I don't know.'

'You did remind him, didn't you?'

'Course I did, I always do what I'm told,' and he grinned at me. I didn't smile back, Sister Hilary had nearly reached us. She was shaking hands with everyone, smiling her rather sweet professionals-only smile.

'Ah, doctor,' she said to Stephen, 'how nice of you to come.'

'Wouldn't have missed it for the world,' said Stephen, which made me flush a little, since it might underline Mr Craddock's absence; but then he took her hand and kissed it, and everyone standing nearby looked at one another and smiled and breathed out, Ah!

'Everybody's been so kind, such a lovely party, I was hardly expecting such a feast! Thank you so much for my delightful presents.'

I glanced over her head as she spoke and to my surprise saw another familiar face: the fat doctoral research student, whose toes had so impressed me all those years before, was standing over by the curtained French windows, looking a bit glum and twiddling an empty sherry glass. I felt quite furious for a moment, seeing her as some kind of gentle Mme Defarge, earnestly knitting while poor old Sister Hilary, in her neat new shoes, was helped up onto the guillotine; pictured myself going over to her and saying venomously, What you doing here? before I remembered that she was fairly high up in the nursing school and probably hadn't had that much choice about coming. And she clearly wasn't gloating anyway. Perhaps she had always known it had just been a question of time: the old queen was on the way out, and the new republicanism of the Nursing Process was on the way in.

'And you, Staff Nurse. I've so enjoyed working with you.'

I shook Sister Hilary's hand. 'Me, too.'

Not once, I thought, has she ever used my proper name. I'd never used hers either.

'And you must come by, sometime, and tell me how you're getting on with your midwifery.'

A polite invitation, not meant, of course. It struck me that she might thus be telling herself, and me, that the earlier one had been bogus too.

'I will,' I promised, and briefly wondered if I should kiss her cheek. I could have done it easily, one hand on her arm, lean forward, a quick peck — I hesitated too long, our hands parted, there was a short, still moment of awkwardness between us, and then she had passed on. That was the last time I spoke to her. After that night, I never saw her again.

Though I've thought of her now and then, especially lately. Staff nurse, midwife, sister: I've brewed a good many of those post-ward-round cups of tea myself, while the conversation has centred round that special endless soap opera, sad, astonishing, frightening, comic: our patients.

'Oh, doctor, were you able to speak to Mr Clark?'

'Yes . . . took it very well, I thought . . .'

'. . . She's simply got no idea, I'm afraid, but I think really she may not want to know, I think that's what it might be . . .'

'. . . She was protecting him, you see, and herself, she was protecting herself from his horror, that's why she wouldn't let him in . . .'

'. . . Yes, three of them, and the youngest's not a year old yet . . .'

'. . . Frightened the poor little student half to death . . .'

'. . . full of little holes, drilled by the equally mad people upstairs!'

I've often wondered if our patients realize to what degree we fictionalize them. Perhaps they suspect, lie there listening to the soft buzz of our talk at the nurses' station by night, or in the office by day, and feel themselves discussed. No, I'm sure they suspect. After all, they fictionalize us in return, watch television's medicated soap operas, Dr Kildare, Angels, Dr Finlay, read all those hospital romances. Mills and Boon could use another title: not *Doctor Nurse Romance* but *The Patients' Revenge*.

'. . . Opened him up and bam it's last rites and telling his mum he won't last the night . . .'

'. . . No, it just collapsed, I'd never seen anything like it . . .'

Strong entertainment, for us to try our nerves on, or impress our friends with. Strong entertainment: the only theatre in which the audience can dry its own cathartic tears and then step smartly up onto the stage with painkillers, blankets, and practised words of comfort. You may tend to feel you're always up there on the stage yourself, when you're first starting your training, but you soon learn where the curtain falls, and that you can and should keep to the right side of it: you're no good to anyone with your hanky constantly held before your eyes.

So, we watch them, and they watch us; we fictionalize them, and they fictionalize us; comfort is sometimes requested, sometimes given. And now and then it all goes wrong, as it did for Sister Hilary. If you're not used to being grown-up yet, if you're shy, nursing can make a good substitute: you don't need to go out and make things happen to you if every day an astonishing array of things is happening to other people, for you to see and, to some extent, to preside over. For years, it must have been enough for Sister Hilary, just to look on, safe in the auditorium. Safe. There's fear at the heart of altruism; a lifetime lived for others means getting the others to do the living for you. But suppose that, as you grew older, you outgrew your anxiety, and found that watching others wasn't really enough after all?

How old was Sister Hilary, when she began to grow jealous of her patients, because the glamour of narrative force chose them and not her? Real things happened to them, shocked and changed and frightened them; she saw these things every day, and yet none of them were happening to her. And she'd been watching for so long; it would be too late by then to realize that, though her patients were being looked after, they hadn't stopped looking back. When they looked back at her they would see a mystifying personal resentment, and they couldn't have taken comfort from her then, even if she had had any left to give.

And all the time the low pay, the wretchedly unsociable hours, the constant procession of ever-younger super-qualified children ...

'... She's a psychopath,' said Stephen as we walked away after the party.

'Perhaps I'll get like that one day,' I said.

'Don't be daft,' said Stephen, 'whyever should you?' He put his arm round me. 'Whyever should you?'

I didn't answer. I was thinking: he's rather a risk. Is he a risk worth taking, my ticket up into the limelight? Anything was better than getting like Sister Hilary.

'I can see how I might.'

'Come off it. You're too good-looking for a start.' He grinned down at me, but his eyes were a little anxious.

I saw then that he didn't want me to think or say anything that he might not be able to understand. I should have disapproved of this, but I made an effort not to. Because, while it wasn't exactly a major factor, I'd seen television's medicated soap operas myself, felt my fictionalized patients fictionalizing me: and he was the doctor and I the nurse.

There. I smiled at him, playing Sister Hilary after all: mentally straightening a few beds for him.

Though of course I didn't see that at the time. I reached up, and kissed him; and then we went home.

INSIDE
KNOWLEDGE

I WAS a patient myself once. I was in the sick bay, the first time I'd ever been on the wrong side of the hospital sheets. I was a midwifery student at the time.

'... So, have you er done any deliveries without gloves on?' asked the district medical officer. He had a mask on to visit me, I could recognize him only by his glasses as the perfunctory organisation-of-the-health-service lecturer at the midwifery school. He was all decked out in a sterile gown and plastic gloves as well. The gloves had misted up.

'Hmm? Think back. Have you? Done any – '

'Oh, one, I think ... I don't know ...' Two consultants, a senior registrar, a junior houseman and the sick bay Sister had already asked me this. So had the blood-sample lady from the lab, who'd attached me to her syringes very gently and carefully, as if I were an unexploded bomb all primed and booby-trapped.

'Anyway, we should have the results this afternoon. Or tomorrow morning. At the latest,' said the DMO, lacing his misty plastic fingers together. I shut my eyes, hoping that he would go away. I didn't really care which sort of hepatitis I turned out to have. On the whole I rather favoured the fatal kind, so long as it did the job fast.

There are consolations to feeling so ill that you don't care about dying. You never get bored, for instance. For nearly a week after I was admitted I just lay in bed, sleeping occasionally, hardly moving, not thinking, not reading, not listening to the radio. I didn't want to eat. I didn't want to see anyone or talk to anyone. I didn't want anything, and I didn't get bored. Normally, left to myself for more than a few minutes, I'd be casting about for a book to read, or turning the TV on, or carrying the radio from room to room with me. I read an awful lot, that first year of my marriage, I always had a book squeezed into my handbag, I'd acquired tickets for three different libraries. It wasn't just boredom I was staving off, I can see that now, but seeing myself, catching myself out doing the washing-up again, or waiting for my husband to come home and being no star after all, not even a bit-part, but something like a setting, a backdrop, an adman's housewife.

Anyway when you're really ill you don't need to protect

yourself from your own eyes any more. You don't need to present yourself in any way. You're very ill, and that's all you are. It's a relief, being just one thing at a time, feeling just one thing, and knowing what the one thing is. You don't want anything, you don't get bored, you know who you are and what you're feeling: no wonder people remember their illnesses, talk about their operations, and look back on it all with a sort of nostalgia; no wonder convalescence often involves depression, re-shouldered burdens often feel heavier than before.

'It's the infective sort, congratulations!' said the sick bay Sister. I could see she was beaming by the crinkles round her eyes.

'That's great,' I said, and turned over, unimpressed even by reprieve.

'You're beginning to go yellow,' said the sick bay Sister, holding her freckled forearm beside my own, 'you'll soon be feeling better.'

I went yellow, with sickly golden eyes to match, and felt better; I didn't need to read yet, but I started on Radio Four again. A day or so later I was well enough to feel lonely, I was still in isolation and that means the nurses won't drop in too often. I didn't have many visitors either, apart from Stephen and my mother. Once my ex-flatmate rang to say she'd be coming but she never arrived. I meant to ask her why not afterwards but I never got round to it. I wasn't seeing so much of her anyway then, she and Stephen didn't get on very well.

One week in hospital, two; I was watching Open University programmes, and Emmerdale Farm, and the Epilogue. I wasn't allowed to borrow books, I was still judged infectious.

'But not an epidemic,' said the DMO. I wondered if he was disappointed, whether he'd been hoping for a full-blown plague to try his hand on.

'May I?' asked the DMO, waving his misty plastic gloves.

'Er, just a minute ...' I folded back the sheet and let him paddle about over my abdomen. They all did, the two consultants, the senior registrar, the junior houseman. I couldn't see any reason to object.

'Liver edge,' said the DMO, straightening up. He sounded pleased.

I knew about the liver edge, I could feel it myself sometimes.

Disease had made my liver swell up like crying eyes. Just before I was taken to hospital it had got so big that its casing of peritoneum had grown too tight for it, and squeezed it all over, producing a pain quite outside the everyday category of human pains, so I'd had to translate it into something else, and told Stephen, 'It hurts me to take a deep breath, it hurts me to breathe,' which had confused him no end, him being a fairly new junior houseman at the time.

Lots of pains are like that though: the approaching heart attack makes your arm go numb, gallstones give you a sharp ache in the shoulder blades. It's confusing. Why shouldn't gallstones just give you a pain in your gallbladder, why shouldn't your liver give you liver-ache? Pleasures are finite too; climb a high tower, or a steep mountain, and look down, and you'll feel a bounding thrill in your legs, in your tensing calf-muscles; and that's how your legs feel in sexual excitement, in that first-night sexual excitement. You try it, next time you go climbing (or vice versa); you concentrate, you'll see.

On the whole it's a comfort, this realization: that human beings just don't have enough nerve endings to interpret things precisely. It's not our fault we mix everything up, consider pneumonia when our livers are all over the place, confuse desire with affection, feel arm-ache instead of heart-ache. It's not our fault, we're a botched job to start with, that's all it is.

I was thinking this sort of thing already, before I fell ill, because of the course I was doing. All nursing's a crash-course in human frailty but midwifery shows you in what style our frailty starts: like most things reproduction looks well enough in principle and in practice turns out to be one drawback after another.

Why does childbirth have to hurt so much, what good does that do? Why is the place the baby comes out of so small, it's ridiculous, anyone could think of better ways of doing it, frogs have got it easier than us, fish have.

'But sheep die lambing, lambs die,' said Stephen once. His uncle had a farm in Somerset, where one year all his cows had needed Caesarian sections, because he'd shot the wrong semen home and all the calves were too big.

'I bet deer don't,' I'd said, 'I bet zebras don't.' Not that I knew, I was just guessing; but it seemed all too likely to me that only the animals we manipulate, ourselves of course included, could ever run into such gory hopeless disasters. *Do* zebras die in childbirth?

'I bet gorillas don't, I bet dolphins don't.'

'No, I suppose not . . .' said Stephen, yawning. He was very tired all the time in those days, being a junior houseman. He must have been paler than some of his patients and none of his clothes fitted him properly any more.

'I'm sorry, I've just got to go to bed – ' and he'd be asleep before I'd finished the washing-up. We were living in a one-room hospital flat then, with a curtain to divide off the bedroom. I spent most of my evenings in, waiting up for Stephen, listening to the radio or watching TV, usually with a book open on my lap as well. Sometimes I'd have homework to do, I'd sit puzzling over an obstetrics textbook and a female pelvis, a clean dry bony pelvis borrowed from the midwifery school, held together here and there with rivets, like a precious piece of broken china. Each slight curve or indentation of that bony ring, pelvis to sacrum, has a name and a function; memorizing these landmarks I'd sit for an hour or so, turning these circular bones over and over in my hands like some dumb female Hamlet considering Every-woman.

There are other bones that prove femininity: certain small cranial differences, variations in tooth insertion, decreased fore-head bossing: but the pelvis speaks clearest, that thorny female crown of bone. The first thing that strikes you is the size: it's so small, it's so bloody small! Forget about the bits you can feel, if you're thin enough, at your own hips, they don't count, appearances really don't count when it comes to childbirth. Forget the child-bearing hips: those bits don't count.

What counts is the internal pelvis, which you can see only on dangerously gonad-frying X-rays, or post-mortem, in the bony pelvis itself: the internal passage, a room with no view but two doors, entrance and exit.

Enter head-first please, a foetal diver, through the pelvic inlet, the first bony doorway, the entrance. It's oval in shape, so enter it sideways, it fits better. Squeezed along by contractions (imagine forcing a golf ball through a length of garden hosepipe) proceed into the pelvic cavity, birth's dark anteroom. It's round, you can't get through it without rotating. Don't get stuck! Or Mum gets a section and so do you. Don't get stuck, rotate towards the exit, the pelvic outlet. Not oval, not round, of course not: diamond-shaped. Turn again baby. Don't get stuck! Or Mum gets forceps, and so do you. Don't get stuck. Stay flexed, stay calm, and there you are: born.

Not exactly Bob's-your-uncle, is it? Why does it have to be so complicated? What's the point of all that geometry? No wonder it all takes so long, no wonder it hurts so much.

You can hold the female bony pelvis in your two wondering hands and note all the specialized flutings and convexities designed to help the baby in, through and out; you can admire their smoothness, their special curving human grace; and you can't help asking yourself why? Why stop there? Why allow so little leeway all round? Why so stingy? Why not smaller passengers or wider tunnels, look at the way supermarket aisles have got wider and wider over the years, why are our insides so poky, so hideously cheese-paring, so cramped?

We're a botched job, that's why. We're a mess. We're accident-prone. Why can the foetus somersault, and knot up its oxygen supply, and so die if the knot should tighten? Or, why should the cord be long enough to wrap twice round the baby's neck? That happens often, it's something you always check for. It can be dealt with, it's not so bad. But if the mother was alone, the child would strangle. Do baby zebras strangle like that, do gorillas?

No, it's only us, and all the other animals we've interfered with. A botch-up. On all levels. Is it my arm that's strained, or is it my heart? Is it my lungs that hurt, or my liver? Do I really want a baby, or am I just jealous of my patients?

Or is it both? Liver *and* lights, jealous *and* broody? Things do overlap so. Events overlap.

I lay in hospital, yellow and fractious; and Stephen's mother, who'd never been ill but for those two brief occasions when Stephen and his sister botched their too-tight way out of her, who'd been, so far as anyone knew, in the very pink of health, unlike her sickly golden daughter-in-law, went to bed one night, went to sleep with her curlers in, and never woke up again, but lay and cooled all night beside her husband, in one long last lie-in.

Well, no. I hadn't liked her. I hardly knew her, but I knew she'd never liked me. She didn't think I was up to much; I was afraid she was right. She never volunteered anything about

herself. I don't think I ever invited her to. I saw her only as
authority, a senior face that disapproved. I was no daughter to
her. Her fault, and mine; a pity all round. Rather a botched job,
in fact.

Anyway she died, very suddenly. Stephen had to go to her
funeral without me, I was still in isolation. He came back feverish
and anorexic, his urine was full of bilirubin; his liver was all over
the place, but it felt like grief. He had hepatitis, of course, but
mildly. They let him visit me after a few days. I put my yellow
arms round his mildly jaundiced neck. He never shed a tear, not
one, but he had dreams.

'You were shouting.'

'Was I?'

'Yes, come on, what were you dreaming about, try to
remember.'

'I can't, it's gone.'

We were on two weeks' holiday, both of us shaky and con-
valescent. He wouldn't talk about his mother.

'I mean, do you feel guilty? That it was her heart, and you
never suspected?'

A massive heart attack; had her right arm ached as she rolled
each curler home that last evening? Hardly the sort of thing
you'd bother a doctor with, a stray ache at night, even if the
doctor was your own son, and rang you once a week.

'No. No one could've known. She hadn't got any symptoms.
I don't want to talk about it, no really, I don't want to talk about
it.'

He had a photograph of her in his wallet, nice tweed skirt,
sensible shoes, row of pearls like the Queen, sitting in her rock
garden, smiling for her son. He hardly spoke of her all that
fortnight, except once, one suppertime, when he remarked on
her light hand with pastry, an unthinking remark. I remember
looking up automatically to meet his eyes, and him not looking
back, not realizing, simply not remembering that she was dead.
It was me who thought, Ah, but she'll never make her pastry
again; me, not her son. So once or twice I found myself suspect-
ing him, that it wasn't so much grief he was controlling as
indifference. I didn't like thinking this about him and presently

came up with more palatable smoothing-over thoughts: This is His Way of Dealing with It and He is Coping. These are smoothing-over thoughts, that make part-sense of pain and confusion. It's the part that's made nonsense of that you then have to ignore, but that's the price you pay if you want any smoothness at all. I always opted for smoothness in those days; it goes with reading six books a week, with the radio on.

Things went on overlapping. When we arrived back in our cramped hospital flat there was a letter waiting for Stephen, a letter informing him that his application for a year's surprisingly well-paid trainee-research job somewhere forgettable in Canada had been successful, that we were to leave that spring, that we would be provided with rent-free hospital accommodation, with carpets, garburetor, and drapes included.

'What's a garburetor?'

'How the hell should I know?'

'Oh –'

'No, I'm sorry. Sorry. It's my dad –'

'Of course –'

'I mean, what with Julia too –'

Stephen's sister had married an Australian she'd met at Durham University, and emigrated to New South Wales. Her children grew in abrupt fits and starts, I'd seen all the photographs. She'd come alone to her mother's funeral, as Stephen had, and gowned up later to visit me, and, as it turned out, Stephen as well.

'You guys look related!' she'd said through her mask, crinkling her eyes at our matching pale-yellow faces. Certainly she hardly looked one of the family herself any more, with her deep healthy-looking tan and sun-blonde hair. She didn't sound like Stephen at all either, she sounded like an Australian trying to speak BBC; she sounded foreign, and looked it too. She never put her arms round Stephen, at least she didn't when I was there. She didn't even kiss him goodbye, though perhaps that was because he might have still been infectious, and she had her three Australian children to think of. All the same, she might not be seeing her only brother again for years to come. I decided that I would've risked it, if I'd been her. But then Stephen didn't touch her either. There was something rather chilling in their detached friendliness. I couldn't imagine Julia crying for her mother either.

I put this down to the mother's coldness, which was all she'd ever shown me, and saw Stephen's controlled secrecy as the result of a childhood short on caresses. I liked feeling sorry for Stephen. I often did. Poor Stephen, I thought then, watching this politely friendly brother and sister. Poor Stephen, loved, but not luxuriously, loved wisely but not too well. It explained a lot, I thought.

'I mean, what with Julia too – '

'Can we postpone it?'

'Well. I don't know. I suppose I could try . . .'

'Or leave it altogether, for the time being?'

(I wasn't too keen on Canada. It didn't seem different enough. I'd said, If we're going abroad, can't we go somewhere really different, somewhere really foreign? It's only for a year, Stephen had said, and look at the money.)

But Stephen's father, applied to, didn't favour either option. We went up to visit him on Stephen's next weekend off. By that time the mother had been dead for nearly two months. The house at first sight looked unchanged. It was a rather beautiful Georgian country house, with furniture to match, all gathered slowly over the years, so Stephen had told me; the dressers held splendid sets of china all complete, pieces of old silver glittered from the tops of the inlaid corner cupboards, a collection of enamelled snuff-boxes simply lay about on the end-table in the drawing-room. And there was so much space; there was a whole room, practically, just to put coats and boots in, and a separate dining-room with a long glossy table to reflect the room's allotment of china, antique silver, and bright cut glass. All the rooms had an undisturbed look, and a calm clean smell of furniture polish and lemon oil. I remembered the first time Stephen had taken me there on a visit. I'd never seen anything like it. Not without having to buy a ticket to get in, anyway.

With Stephen's mother dead the rooms looked almost the same at first, but after a while I realized that their undisturbed look was now genuine, arose from under-use rather than from detailed attention. Mr Dalton was practically living in the kitchen. In our honour he opened up the drawing-room to give us tea in, and the room smelt museum-musty, and the snuff-boxes and a few other small bits of silver, little vases and jugs and so on, had all vanished, stowed away in cupboards.

'Jeannie Holroyd still comes in twice a week,' said Mr Dalton, carrying in a loaded tea-tray. I noticed a shop-bought cake, biscuits still in the packet. 'Don't know where I'd be without her.'

I'd met Jeannie Holroyd once. Stephen's mother called her Jeannie, she called Stephen's mother Mrs Dalton. So did I. Jeannie was a young shaggy-haired blonde. The one time I'd met her she'd hardly looked up from the stairs, where she was furiously polishing the stair-rods, though I felt her eyes hard on my back as I passed into the kitchen where Mrs Dalton was sitting over the day's consignment of silver. The kitchen door was open, I imagined so that Mrs Dalton could keep an eye on Jeannie's polishing while she rubbed up the silver. I'd offered to help, and Mrs Dalton had looked up, pausing, pink-rubbered fingers splayed out over a rather gnarled and dumpy sauceboat, remarked on my kindness, and said that she preferred to do the silver herself, and I went away crushed. Perhaps rather more crushed than she'd intended. Well, I overestimated her strength too, I can see that now.

'But really the place is too much for me,' said Mr Dalton, pouring out the tea. I asked him if he was thinking of moving, and he told me to call him Geoffrey, and that he hadn't rightly thought of the future at all yet, which gave Stephen an opening to explain about the Canadian job.

'I just don't like leaving you here,' said Stephen finally. He looked as if he were in pain while he was speaking, but all the way in the car he'd seemed much happier than usual, almost excited with happiness, exalted. Even as he spoke now, painfully, there was a faint glow of this exaltation behind his voice. He looked at his father with what seemed to be pride.

'I can't just leave you here.'

'Oh, you mustn't worry about me, I'll be all right,' said Geoffrey. 'Here, let me top you up ...' He sounded almost jaunty. I thought that he was rather enjoying himself, playing houses, that it was a novelty for him to see to himself and act hostess, and it struck me, really for the first time, that a marriage was not necessarily a happy one simply because it had lasted a long time. I remembered a weekend about eighteen months earlier, Stephen and I still engaged; Geoffrey had asked me if I'd like a bath after the long cold ride up from London, and his wife had corrected his pronunciation, rather sharply.

'Barth, darling, barth, not bath.'

I'd been very surprised at this, not so much because of the attitude it implied, but at the crudity of the attack itself, its double-edged public-ness. I must have done something especially, snivellingly, proletarian to provoke it. I had to make quite strenuous efforts not to look up and catch anyone's eyes, because of course if she felt like that about her husband's mild Yorkshire, what would she really like to say about my slipshod South London? Though she dropped the odd broad A herself now and then. I used to listen out for them.

'It's a grand opportunity for you,' said Geoffrey now, holding out Stephen's refilled tea-cup. 'I don't want you missing out on my account. You go. You please me, you go.'

'I don't know,' said Stephen, looking down. 'I was thinking, you know. Christmas, next Christmas. I know it's daft. But you'll be on your own.' He looked up then. 'I don't want that. I don't want to think of you on your own.'

'Well –' said Geoffrey, sitting back in his chair. Neither of them seemed to know what to say next.

I said, 'Well, couldn't you come out, Geoffrey? I mean, come and visit us, a holiday?'

Everyone smiled and shifted about in their chairs at this, it was so obviously the solution, though Geoffrey had to make a few disclaimers first, about leaving the business, and intruding, and getting in the way, and so on. But it was all settled soon enough, we would go, and he would follow for two weeks at Christmas, and we all felt very pleased with ourselves, especially me, though of course I had no inkling then of the passion with which I would one day look forward to Geoffrey's arrival: not for Geoffrey's own sake, but because of the feel of England he would be bringing with him. But then, I didn't anticipate homesickness.

Stephen disappeared for a few minutes that night while we were getting ready for bed. He came back in holding out a small framed picture.

'Look, it used to hang in Julia's room.'

I looked, and saw a bright summery watercolour, a stretch of dappled greenish water, with a rowing-boat moored in the middle and three men on board, fishing. One wore a hat, and a shaded smile was all you could see of his face. The other two also smiled, faintly, as if they were listening to a story being slowly told, with pauses, by the man beneath the hat. The whole scene looked private, almost secretive, as if the two listeners had agreed beforehand not to pass the story on.

'It's my mother's,' said Stephen, 'my mother did it.'

'What!'

'It was her hobby,' said Stephen.

I looked again at the bright greenish water, the listening smiles. I felt rather appalled: baffled, misled. I'd thought she'd spent all her time cleaning and acquiring.

'It's very good.'

'Yes, yes,' said Stephen, and he wrapped the picture up in the shirt he'd just taken off, and tenderly laid it in our suitcase.

'I'm going to take it with us,' he told me.

I lay in bed thinking that I'd soon get used to it and stop seeing it. I told myself that I had other, bigger things to worry about, a foreign country, a new job, no one to fall back on. Except Stephen, of course.

'That's nice,' I said, 'good idea.'

The place was called Tabor. Tabor was a boom-town; the buildings were as young as its population, and set in a gridwork of wide numbered streets. It was hard to take a walk in Tabor, the roads all went the long way round, they flew-over, they by-passed; they hadn't grown from ancient footpaths, they had been intelligently designed for the comfortable passage of sleek feline American cars.

In the city centre a thicket of skyscrapers crammed the air; by daylight they seemed to hold their breath, so great was the suggestion of strain about their glass or mirrored sides. In summer, like a forest of towering sundials, they all cast shade upon each other, you beetled past their massive bases through shifting bars of sharp-edged shade a whole street wide, so that the sun winked even at noon. Contrasted to their glittering sunlit sides their shaded bases looked chilly and dank, their human-size doorways like a reluctant afterthought.

At night, though, they swopped characters, their tiers of windows glowed and sparkled with bright golden lights; seen from our own apartment a mile or so away the towers by night were suddenly all nostalgic Hollywood America, a glittering black-and-white city where innocent dancing-girls tapped their way down 42nd Street, and Philip Marlowe waited in alleys, with his trench-coat collar turned up and his hat brim tilted down. At night Tabor looked familiar.

By day I could only think of it as a place to drive away from, but there was nowhere to drive to, only more places just the same, set at intervals in the flat burnt-brown prairies, along roads so straight that they reached an optical infinity, and met in a faint blue haze.

I bought a car in Tabor, the first I'd ever owned. Stephen bought one as well; hard to do otherwise in a city designed to be driven in. Stephen had more money than me and bought a little sporty car, but I bought an elderly battered Chevrolet. It felt about as wide as a double-decker bus, and as safe as a tank to drive. I never got used to its size and knocked it into things, lampposts and bollards, about every other week. I kept a can of paint in the trunk for quick repairs. Oh, I'm sorry, I would whisper to my Chevrolet as I sprayed over the latest dented graze, Oh, I am sorry . . .

Several times that first summer I just got into it and drove around, through the crowded acres of creamy new 'luxury homes', just-built or half-built all about the city, along the six-lane highways past the centre, and out onto the gravelled intersecting country roads to nowhere in particular, trailing a greyish-yellow plume of dust behind me for mile after mile after mile.

'Where on earth have you been?'

'Oh, nowhere really, just out for a ride.'

Our apartment in Tabor had large sealed double-glazed windows through which the Hollywood backdrop city romantically gleamed at night, through which the sun beat brightly by day. It was on the tenth floor, air-conditioned, centrally-heated, humidified.

'It's convenient for work and it's rent-free.'

'Well I wish there was a balcony. I wish I could just stick my hand out of the window, I can't tell what the weather's like.'

'You can look out and see what people are wearing, then you'll know.'

But I couldn't; there were hardly ever any people in sight, they were all inside their cars.

'It hardly matters does it? I mean, you can use the tunnel anyway.'

There was an underground corridor between our apartment building's basement garage and the hospital. We could go to work and back without once seeing the sky.

'Handy now it's getting colder.'

I liked the new cold, that properly foreign extreme. At twenty below, the air freezes the little hairs in your nostrils, they stiffen and prickle; it feels as if someone were very gently poking a Brillo pad up your nose. Meanwhile your eyelashes grow a heavy white mascara of frost, and jokily stick together, and your woollen balaclava turns to bendy cardboard over your lips.

Once, ski-ing over the flat parkland beside the frozen river, I developed a mild frostbite: two toes temporarily white and dead. I was astonished. There I'd been, quite happily poling myself along in the bright cold sunshine, chatting of this and that, and all the time my body had been struggling against the overwhelming odds of a twenty-five below, and desperately deciding to sacrifice two toes to the greater good, the two toes meekly submitting to the preliminary processes of execution without so much as a twinge of protest.

Frostbite! It was so thrillingly foreign. I boasted about it in my letters home. All the same it was disconcerting, at least as disconcerting as mistaking your liver for your lungs. How could all that have gone on without my knowing it? And if my body was capable of jettisoning bits of itself without so much as a by-your-leave, what else was it capable of? What else might it try for, without my knowledge?

'No. Not now. Not yet.'

'Why not? Oh, why not, we've been married more than a year, don't you want one?'

I never said I did. I never said it out loud, not at first. It was still connected in my mind with failure, with having given up on yourself. I wanted it to happen by accident, I wanted Stephen to want it to happen. I didn't push; I told myself this was strategy.

But it was on my mind, more and more. I couldn't really escape it, my work permit said obstetric nurse and that was all I could be, an obstetric nurse or unemployed. The thought of unemployment made me remember those long straight dusty roads, waiting for me, holding out infinity like the rainbow's end.

So I kept working: unit 47, Tabor General, the labour ward.

'D'you have any children yourself?'

'Well, no, actually . . .'

'Guess all this puts you off, right?'

Nearly all my patients got round to asking me such things. Occasionally labour really cracks along fast, or someone comes in ready to deliver straight away; but usually there's a twelve-to-sixteen hour stretch of it, longer sometimes. Often I'd attend someone on labour-inducing drugs all one late shift, switch her off at night, and turn her on again in the morning for another day's trial.

So there was a lot of time to pass; and at the beginning, while my patient would still be at the stage of thinking that it was really much more painful than she thought it would be, but that she could stand it, she'd ask me questions, we'd chat. I always had a lot of explaining to do; it was a high-tech place, Tabor General.

'See, it measures the contractions up here, these sort of mountains show the wave of the contraction, up to the peak, down again, this one's the baby's heartbeat . . .'

Most of the labours at Tabor were induced or made faster by feeding the woman Syntocinon through an intravenous line. My job was to sit beside her, turning up the flow every fifteen minutes or so, inducing sharper contractions and thus greater pain, pencilling the dosages on the monitor-tracing.

Up 20

Up 10

Down 10

And so on, counting with her through the contractions, fifteen, sixteen, seventeen, peaking now Susan, keep breathing, twenty, twenty-one, twenty-two, easing now, that's good, very good, and bringing a cold wet flannel for her forehead, holding her hand, pencilling on the tracing again:

Demerol 25mg IV 14.10 or

Epidural test-dose 15.35.

Presiding over dissolution while the mysterious inner compartments stretched, gave and opened, or balefully stayed shut no matter what pain the drugs produced. There's no machine to monitor those fleshy inner doors as yet; just the midwife's fingers, my fingers, as gentle as I could make them.

'That's it, relax as much as you can – '

Very gently, I part the outer lips, careful not to fold them painfully inwards as my fingers slide between, and very slowly press up through that warm wet two-way passage. I remember the first time I did this, as a student midwife, how startled I'd been: everything felt so unfamiliar. It didn't feel anything like my own non-matronly insides, encountered in the cause of curiosity and contraception. Labouring women feel completely different, everything that was firm and resilient has turned to a tender anticipatory mush, unrecognizably yielding and slithery, that only experience can make sense of.

Now my qualified practised fingers measure buried prominences of bone to calculate available space, they reach up through the soft straining bag of membranes before the baby's head to note a landmark suture line or fontanelle, and measure the cervix effacing, dilating, or stubbornly not doing anything at all.

'I'd like to break the membranes now actually, Mrs Verensky, I think that will speed things up for us – '

Peel the Amnihook out of its sterile packet, thread its plastic snaky button-hook head through and up, catch, pull and

'Oh God, is that the waters? Oh God – '

'Yes, everything's fine, it didn't hurt, did it? No, and everything's fine, lovely and clear – ' or sometimes not. Sometimes the waters pour out dingy, yellow or brownish, because the baby, like all creatures in physical dread, has opened its bowels, and its pure tarry little shits have stained the flow. There were rules to follow in such cases.

'Well, we need to have a better tracing of the baby's heartbeat now Helen, because, see? this colour shows that the baby's been under some stress, it's nothing to worry about but it's a sign, d'you see, that we need to keep an extra close eye on him – '

And Baby gets an electrode pinned to his head, screwed into his scalp on a curled steel needle.

'Very good, he's looking very good . . . ' or sometimes,

'Well now, I'm just going to switch the drip off for a bit, give this baby a rest, see, just a little while,' because the monitor's begun registering the special swooping patterns babies' heartbeats go in for just before they give out altogether.

'Back in a moment,' I say lightly at the door, and break into a run for the telephone down the corridor.

'Hallo? Yes, it's Mrs Appleby. Type Twos. I have. Right. Thanks,' sprint back and smile in the doorway.

'Ah, Dr Brown'll be popping in to see you in a moment – '

There was a whole crowd of doctors at Tabor General. Obstetric nurses weren't supposed to deliver the babies, we had to call each patient's doctor, who'd rush in at the last minute, usually, to take charge. It was like running a special race every day, leading all the way, and then having to stand aside at the end, to let someone else win it. The someone else, the doctor, being in nearly every case a man, prone to call his patients sweetheart and to insist on all the paraphernalia of American childbirth; masks, sterile gloves, an atmosphere of controlled hysteria, bright lights, strident yells of command, forceps and dorsal lithotomy.

It's so much easier to be angry on someone else's behalf than on your own. So I found it. I was constantly arguing, at work. Why strap women flat on their backs with their feet in the air, it's ridiculous! Why do a mid-line episiotomy when they extend into the rectum? How d'you *know* a rectal tear doesn't matter, doctor, are there any surveys to prove that? Why do a pudendal block every time, doctor? They stop women wanting to push, what's the point? Doctor? What's the point?

I knew what the point was. The point was control. Strap a woman into dorsal lithotomy, paralyse her with Amethocaine, and you'd be at least partly in control, of that terrifying messy unpredictable botch-up, a natural birth. And doctors don't sit beside their labouring patients, they don't witness the inexorable process of dissolution-through-pain. One day Dr Brown would see Mrs Sinclair waiting in his office, neat and composed for her final check-up; the next he'd be tearing into the hospital to take charge of an expulsion, a bloodied forced exit, a spread screaming pair of legs: no wonder he was so frightened.

Yet charge must be taken, so use drugs, use force, use stentorian shouts, use terror: use your own.

'I think they're actually frightened. D'you think they're frightened?' I asked Beryl Best one day on our coffee break. Beryl was a year older than me, unmarried, and childless. I liked Beryl.

'Sure I think they're frightened. They're also real bastards.' I laughed, but she said, 'Listen. Male obstetricians: they either simply love women, or they not-at-all-simply hate them. The ones that love them are all right. The ones that hate them, you watch out. You know who I mean. Right?'

I knew. Ah, Dr Phelan, I can see you now, haggard, loose-mouthed, leaning against the nurses' station to talk investments with a junior, or standing in the delivery room, rubber gauntlets bloodied to the elbow, manually removing the placenta without an anaesthetic, manfully deaf to shrieks and pleas.

'But they come back for more,' said Beryl Best, 'not all his patients are first-timers.'

'Well, if they don't know any different – '

'Oh come on. Would you go back to him for number two?'

'No, but – '

'Look, you know, I think women get what they ask for. Or they ask for what they get. Whatever. Don't you think your job is to protect them? From the doctor? I mean, you know what's going on. You protect the patient from the doctor, as far as you can. Isn't that what you do in England?'

I thought about it. 'I don't think so. Not so much. Well, I mean, they're not around so much.'

'It's not so obvious.'

'What, the war between men and women? No, perhaps not.' I smiled. Actually I was feeling miserable that day. Stephen and I had rowed the previous evening, starting off about who should've done the washing-up and branching out to include almost everything. I'd locked myself in the bathroom, I don't really know why. Stephen had slept on the couch. I felt low the next day but at the time I'd almost enjoyed it, all that shouting, making Stephen shout back at me through the bathroom door. It felt like real life.

Sometimes our apartment with its night-time Hollywood-city windows felt about as real as a cardboard stage set. I couldn't get to grips with it, it felt more alien to me than unit 47, where I was so angry all the time. And Stephen himself seemed shadowy, often, a shadow I went shopping with or accompanied to the pictures, and who could hardly be expected to understand what I was so angry about.

'You like being a foreigner!' I'd screamed through the bathroom door. I was almost sure he wanted to stay in Canada, was angling for a permanent job. He'd never said so, but I was afraid to ask out-right, in case he said yes.

'It's an excuse to you, it explains you, you *like* being a foreigner!'

'Maybe we can help a few little changes along,' said Beryl Best next day in the coffee room, 'but nothing fundamental. It's all like, tied in, with bigger things.' She looked irritated. She waved her hands, groping: 'You can't change things, not this way round. Yeah?'

No, I thought, no no no. I went on trying. I read up every obstetrical journal I could find, made notes, remembered statistics.

'Did you realize that the supine position impairs circulation, causing hypotension and decreased urinary output?'

'Well, yes, but –'

'Did you know that squatting increases the pelvic outlet by 1.5 cm ? Did you?'

That was a good one, I thought. It made me remember those quiet evenings in London, Stephen asleep on one side of the curtain, me awake on the other, peering into a textbook and that complex circle of bone. 1.5 cm . . . it seemed hard to imagine that bone could be so stretchy. But bones you hold in your hands are always dead, as dead as dinosaur bones all turned to stone. They wouldn't be like that living. They can move, stretch, strain their ligaments, expand under pressure: doors of bone opening. Both must open, doors of bone and doors of flesh, but which moved first? Did flesh move bone, or bone flesh? The more I found out, the more abstruse and puzzling the whole process became: squat properly, heels on the ground, and your bony pelvis opens up a full 1.5 cm more, a world of difference in a botched job. Did gorillas squat in labour?

'Well dolphins don't, do they, zebras don't.'

Beryl and I giggle in the coffee room.

'I mean, have you ever *tried* squatting like that, I mean, come on!'

'All right then, but did you know that standing can reduce the length of the first stage by up to a third?'

The trouble was that even those who would stay still and listen to all this had heard it already, the younger doctors had heard or read it already. But no one wanted to apply it.

'You can't monitor someone who's standing up,' said nice Dr Elsdon, 'you couldn't monitor anyone that *squatted*.' Even he made squatting sound rather disgustingly faecal. But I ignored this revealing sideswipe.

'If they stood up, if they were squatting, maybe we wouldn't need to monitor them.'

'Maybe. You want to take the risk? With someone else's kid? Brain damage is irrevocable. You want to risk that?'

'It's because they're all men,' I told Beryl Best in the bar one night. 'That's why they won't listen to me.'

'Oh yeah? You heard of the guy who discovered vitamin C beat scurvy? He finds out limes and stuff beat scurvy. Irrefutable. He tells the British Navy. You know when the Navy takes it up, officially? Forty years later. A year after the guy's died! Forty years! That's a whole bunch of scurvy, kid,' said Beryl Best.

'Well the Navy, the bloody Navy, they were all men too, weren't they?'

Beryl looked hard at me then, not smiling. I looked back, uncertain. I didn't know how far I was joking, either. She stood up.

'You want another beer?' asked Beryl.

But it was Ginette Derby that made me change my tactics: just in time, probably, people were beginning to remember urgent appointments whenever I caught them looking at all accessible.

I looked after Ginette Derby just before Christmas, a week or so before Geoffrey was due to arrive. She was hurtled in by ambulance in premature labour, I just had time to get everything ready for her, same machinery, different drugs, all to stop the contractions this time, to keep the doors closed when they were trying to open. But we didn't need them, drugs or machines, because the baby was dead, dead for some time, said Dr Elsdon to me in the corridor as he wheeled the portable ultrasound back towards the lift. I said I'd call him, he said, Anytime.

I went back to Mrs Derby, Ginette by then, I'd been with her nearly an hour already, and brought her a fresh box of Kleenex.

'I'm sorry,' she said, 'I just can't seem to stop,' and the thought of not being able to stop crying made her cry all the more, as if she had seen herself from the outside, a woman who'd lost a baby, and was crying out of pity, and for someone else. She stopped after a while though, and we chatted a little, about whether she could eat anything, and how soon she'd be able to go home, and how much she missed her children.

'Is my purse there?'

'Here.'

She opened it, rummaged inside.

'Oh, mind the drip –'

'Sorry –'

'It doesn't matter, I mean, it'd be awful if you dislodged it, I'd have to put another one in, you see.'

'Yes, yes. Here, look.'

Two photographs. They made me remember my sister-in-law Julia's Australian children, whom I'd only seen in photographs, still abruptly altering with the letters she sent us every couple of months or so.

'They're very pretty. This one's Martin?'

'And that's Jane. She's eighteen months now. Never stops talking.'

'You'll be back home really soon,' I said.

She lay back, dabbing at her eyes.

'I guess England's really home for you still, is it?'

So I talked for a bit about homesickness and the odd things I found myself missing most. I even made her laugh once or twice.

'No really, post offices there have this special smell, sort of sweet very old paper, and there's always all these ancient posters all over the walls, all faded . . .'

I diverted her. There were other things that I didn't say to her. They were things it would be unthinkable to say. I didn't dream of saying them, please understand that. It's just that I was aware of them:

What's so terrible, you've got two already, haven't you?

What's the problem, you can get pregnant again next month, can't you?

And I'm six years older than you and I haven't got any children at all, and my husband says he doesn't want any, not yet, not yet, and when I finally said When, he said Maybe never, maybe never, so what's so terrible, lady, what's your problem?

No, I never thought of saying those things, of course I didn't. My awareness of them made me, if anything, more anxious than ever to be all that she could ask for in a nurse. And so I was, I know it: kind, diverting, gentle.

I only examined her once. The membranes had been broken so long; poke about too often through ruptured membranes and you're asking for trouble. I waited. She wasn't on any monitor, I just left my hand on her abdomen to see if the contractions were still going strong, it was like the old days at my training hospital, where the consultant in charge had scorned machines and preached Leboyer. It was quiet in that room, Ginette sleepy by now with Demerol, no foetal heartbeat to worry about; the next-to-worst thing had happened already, no blame attachable. I'd drawn the curtains. It was almost peaceful.

'Oh God!' cried Ginette, sitting up fast. I jumped in my chair, but my voice was calm, on automatic, 'What is it?'

'It's coming, it's coming! Oh my God!'

'Lie back, don't be frightened, let's hope it's nearly over, just a moment –'

I wash my hands fast in the bathroom, I don't want her delivering too fast, I want the doctor here, prem. labours bleed.

'Put your knees up now, let them fall apart, that's very good –'

Into that alien familiar country, known only by touch, moving along, taking note automatically:

external genitalia normal

vagina warm and moist

cervix effaced, but

Christ what's this, *Christ* what is it? I take my hand away smoothly. I haven't hurt her very much. (I never hurt anyone very much. I never tell them it won't hurt at all. I'm too good for that.)

'I'm going to call Dr Elsdon, you're just about ready. Try not to push. It doesn't matter too much if you can't help it; but try not to, okay?'

A nod.

'I'll be about a minute.'

Skid round the corner, dash for the phone.

'Doctor? Doctor!'

Well, he was nice, that Dr Elsdon, all in his greens before I'd finished unpacking the delivery trolley and transferred poor Ginette, crying again, to the delivery table where her first child, pretty Martin, had been born, so she told me.

'Oh no. It's the only one free, I'm so sorry –'

'It doesn't matter, I'm being silly –'

'No, of course you're not, of course you're not –'

All the while I was tearing packs open, tying gown-strings, lighting the lamps. All set? Lights? Action – '

'Here we go,' said Dr Elsdon, 'that's very good, just a little push now, just a little one . . .'

It had been the baby's feet I'd felt, almost unrecognizable, puffed by death into strange dintable shapes. Babies that die *in utero* undergo a strange process of sterile corruption, as saints might in their tombs; pockets of gas form, the brains liquefy; not a sea-change, but a uterine change, a pure decay within those quiet waters.

'Just a little push now, just a little one – '

The feet had been bruised against the cervix; the rest of the body flowed out hardly distorted, a slender perfect male child, caught now only by its head.

'Nearly there,' I said to Ginette, whose nails were leaving crescents in my palm, 'nearly there.'

And then she was there: the head came free. As it passed through those doors it emptied, squeezed by parturition; the face, whole for a second, flattened and distended as the structures beneath it collapsed, rocked as if with life as it drained, sank, became two-dimensional.

I had thought myself immune by now. But for a moment I was dizzy with horror. Just for a moment, then I could look away, look up at Ginette. I saw her anguished face. She hadn't seen what had happened. She was possessed by crisis but not by the horror; by the crisis of her pain and loss. I took a sterile cloth from the trolley, and laid it over the body between her legs, hiding it while I thought out a way of getting it off the table without her realizing its nature.

'Er, did you happen to ask her if she wanted to see it? You know?'

Dr Elsdon asked me, leaning towards me and whispering through his mask.

'Yes. She said she didn't.'

He rolled his eyes at me, implying Thank God. I nodded.

That was Ginette Derby. She went home the next day, or the day after. I thought about her a lot, or rather, about what I had seen: that, after the first shock, it hadn't really bothered me. It had been for her sake that I'd covered it, not my own or Dr Elsdon's. I felt that the event had been correctly shared out, and was thus bearable for everyone: hers the loss, mine, as attendant, the horror. It wasn't my baby, my loss, so I could take the horror. If such a disaster was ever my turn, someone else would take the horror, I would have the loss.

I saw that this was what my job was, that this was an honourable task, and that the rest was detail; that in the light of this central serenity, I need not fight so hard.

Anyway I stopped badgering people so much. I hadn't accepted things as they were. But I saw what my own part in them should be. I couldn't change anything but I could foresee the horrors, and damp them down where I could: not liberation, perhaps, but resistance.

'Ah, I expect you've heard about ah pubic shaves?' I would diffidently ask my new patient as she unpacked her suitcase. 'Do you really want one?' And when she'd said Well no, but she'd thought she'd got to have one, I'd say, 'Not at all, unless you *want* one,' and of course she never did, and I'd write in the notes, Refused shave, and that was one ritual humiliation less, as well as one in the eye for Dr Thickhead who'd never read the surveys proving that shaving increased infection instead of reducing it, and who never would, and who never noticed his patients' unshavenness anyway, simply assuming that shaving had taken place since he had decreed it must.

'Twerp,' I'd sneer mentally at Dr Thickhead's back as I meekly tied his theatre gown up. It cheered me up no end.

Several times, too, I didn't call the doctor at all, just pretended everything had happened too fast. I did it twice to butcher Phelan, delivered two of his multips nicely in their labour beds, no rips, no screams, no blood. Lots of fright, though: mine, because I was out of practice as well as strictly in the wrong, and the patients, because both of them thought only doctors could deliver babies, that a baby simply wouldn't be able to come out at all without a doctor to haul it clear at the other end. Still they both did beautifully, and the head nurse gave me a long hard talking-to and Dr Phelan glared (I'd cost him two sets of fees) and I knew I couldn't play that particular game too often, rewarding as it was, if I wanted to stay employed at all.

'Though it sounds like a terrible job to me,' said Geoffrey that Christmas. 'Could you not just pack it in?'

Geoffrey had a lot to say that Christmas.

So why didn't I pack the job in, just shelve all those frights and furies? Well, I liked earning so much money. I was earning as much as Stephen. I liked that. And I couldn't do anything else; it was unit 47 or those long straight dusty roads.

But there was another reason I stayed on: the same old reason, the reason nursing's addictive: the rewards of love, professional but tender, the love that could decently speak its name if only it had one. Real relationships, all of them, for all those women and me. Real but brief. It's odd to think of the number of women who'll remember me for the rest of their lives. There must be at least two hundred of them. They'll never forget me. I'll stay the same for them, my face, my voice, my gentle hands, while they grow older and their children grow up.

It's not really vanity to say so, they'd remember me just as well if I'd been cruel or sarcastic, as Dr Phelan's patients must surely remember him. Perhaps there are a few who remember me that way too; you can hide most troubles but it's hard to stop them chilling your eyes. But on the whole I must've been kind, as kind as I wanted to be. I still have a pile of thank-you cards to prove it, a whole shoeboxful.

Trevor and I just want to thank you once again for all your real caring and expertise ... '

or

Just a small token of our deep appreciation for your great kindness ... '

That sort of thing. Last time I moved bedsits I had a quick look through them and found that I couldn't put a single face to any of the names. Not one. It didn't matter. In a way, this forgetfulness was part of my job, or a result of it. Cards like that used to be pinned to the noticeboard by the nurses' station to be picked up after report. Even at first reading I'd have trouble connecting the signature with a patient, though perhaps less than a week had gone by since the birth. I'd make this quite clear to the other nurses, smiling as I shrugged my shoulders over the latest envelope, flipping through the record book after report to see if anything about the case jogged my memory, and sometimes it did, but more often it didn't.

'Honestly, I just haven't a clue!'

It was something we all did: not to remember our patients added a gloss, somehow, to our expertise, turned what otherwise might have looked like a normal overflow of tenderness and sympathy into a performance, an act of professional piety which had not fully involved our private non-professional selves. You felt pleased when a thank-you card arrived, but especially smug when you couldn't quite remember the woman who'd sent it.

I can see all this partly-willed amnesia as a kind of protection, now. Understand: the doctors were men, the patients were women. Might was right, and Leboyer was wrong. Where did that leave us, the nurses?

It was as if birth, the actual delivery, were reality, the real task. Because birth was real, men undertook it. Which made our eight or twelve hours' close attendance seem less real, a fuss, the conveyor-belt job women usually get stuck with; not a real important task in itself. But the cards were proof that our patients would after all remember us, that they had accepted what we had done for them as something of importance. It was icing on the cake, to have forgotten them: to have done the job well out of sheer professionalism, not out of some suspect female sympathy. Our forgetfulness was a distortion, the product of a place where men were too crudely victorious over women.

So thank you, thank you once again, from Mark and me, and not forgetting little David Alexander, we'll never forget all you did for us . . .

I tried to explain some of this, a necessarily censored account, to Geoffrey when he asked me why I didn't just resign. I even showed him the latest card.

'You see, it has its compensations . . .'

On the whole I was pretty glad to get back to work. Geoffrey's visit hadn't so much changed things as speeded everything up. Stephen's hours at work grew longer and longer. When he was home he spent a lot of time in the bathroom, hours and hours, he'd empty the bath and refill it, the door locked against me.

'Do you still love me?' I'd asked him once despairingly over dinner.

'Of course I do, of course,' he'd said, but when I'd put my hand out to touch his he'd withdrawn it. He had applied for the permanent job, and knew he'd get it.

'And I just don't think I'm ever going to want children. Ever.'

'I see.'

'I'm sorry.'

'So am I.'

'But there it is.'

And there I was. How had this happened, I wondered, how had my vague dreams, the examinations swotted for and passed, the night-shifts stumbled through, the humble pies swallowed, all brought me to this pass, to being nearly thirty, exiled, and childless? It had all felt like progress, but it had been a bumpy rush downhill.

I'd had hopes of Geoffrey's visit. Not only because he'd bring England closer but for other more scheming reasons. I thought his joy at seeing his son again might show Stephen how important it is to have a child to think about in your old age. I meant to use Geoffrey's loneliness. I'd pictured shaking my head at Stephen in private and saying, 'Oh, he's looking a lot older, isn't he,' making sure that Stephen realized for himself where his duty lay, that we must soon go home for good. I could see that this was a classic female role to play, underhand nudging and needling, but since directness had failed it was all I had left, and it was all for the best anyway, or so I told myself.

Though I needn't have bothered with schemes or excuses, I saw that straightaway at the airport. I hardly recognized him at first.

'Dad?' I don't think Stephen did either, for a moment.

'Hallo, you two!' Geoffrey was lightly tanned, springy with fitness and about two stone lighter than before.

'Dad!'

'Oh, it's grand to see you again,' said Geoffrey, briefly embracing his son. He gave me a hug too.

'Hallo,' I said, smiling. I smiled my nurse's smile. 'Hallo, you *do* look well!'

We had a new Resident on unit 47 after Christmas. She'd trained in a province further east. She came to the nurses' coffee room when we were quiet and introduced herself. She spoke of the patients as clients. She'd read Sheila Kitzinger.

'What we all need,' said this new Resident, 'is a kind of obstetrical consumerism.'

I felt very excited listening to all this, my heart beat faster. Not a pure excitement. The new Resident was rather a pretty young woman, blonde, nicely done up in a John Mulloy dress-for-success pinstriped skirted suit and glittering lapel pin.

Later I did a delivery with her, and she used dorsal lithotomy, pudendal anaesthesia, and forceps. Not even Beryl Best could detect what lay behind my eyes then. I didn't want anyone looking too close, myself included.

'I may have got it wrong, that guy with the vitamin C,' said Beryl. 'It wasn't forty years. I was wrong. It was fifty.'

'She's like women politicians,' I said, reasonably, more-in-sorrow-than-in-anger. 'She has to be a better man than they are.'

Cunning, right? But I had to have something, and if I wasn't head of Resistance at work, what was I?

'You know something,' said Beryl after a pause, 'you look awful, you on a diet or what?'

'Of course not. I could do with a holiday though.'

'I thought you just had one,' said Beryl.

Geoffrey had noticed the picture straight away, stopping beside it in our little hallway.

'Hey, isn't that – '

'Yes.' I hadn't stopped seeing it, as I'd thought I would. Though lately I'd begun to imagine that the man in the hat must be telling rather a dirty story, that the listeners weren't smiling so much as smirking.

'Aye well – '

'Come and see our view.'

He recognized the Hollywood night-time city too, I thought.

'Eh, that's grand!'

I felt a bit panicky looking at him. I'd written to him fairly often, he'd written back, we'd spoken several times on the telephone, holding those special long-distance conversations, where both sides first must establish what time it is where, and that judging by the sound they could be half-a-mile apart: achey transatlantic conversations. It wasn't that he didn't look quite real, standing there in our apartment enjoying the backdrop, but that he looked almost

too real, larger than life. He made me think of those giant Donald
Ducks and Mickey Mouses that pad by waving in all the
American city parades.

'Want a drink, Dad?'

We drank icy American beer, Stephen straight from the bottle.
He'd developed quite a few Canadian habits lately. I sat listening
to him describing his office to his father, and thought what a
strange family they were, Yorkshire father, Australian daughter,
Canadian son. More than once I'd found myself correcting
Stephen.

'A lot of people, a great many, not a *whole bunch*!' I'd heard
myself do it. Not bath darling, barth. No wonder the fishermen
were smirking.

'Eh, it's grand to see you two again,' said Geoffrey suddenly
and warmly.

'Great to see you,' rejoined Stephen.

'Especially looking so well,' I said helplessly.

'Aye well, I'll tell you what it is, it's all that jogging I've been
doing. I'm out rain or shine, regular as clockwork, five miles a
day it is now, I only wish I'd started years ago, it makes all the
difference. You could do with summat like that yourself, lad,'
said Geoffrey teasingly to Stephen, and I felt a real hot surge of
anger, that rocked me even though I knew what dank sinful roots
it sprang from. Oh Lord, I thought, some holiday this is going to
be, and I remembered unit 47 and all the horrors there, and felt
suddenly tense enough to scream, to run over to Geoffrey and
slap his clean brown face, to yank Stephen's beer bottle out of his
mouth and hurl it through the wide sealed double-glazed
windows at the winking city beyond.

'I'll just see how the spuds are doing,' I said, perhaps quite
nicely, perhaps with a voiceful of murder, I don't know. Anyway
I went off and stabbed at the potatoes, and after supper Geoffrey
went to bed early, because for him it was nearly dawn really,
'Though I feel great considering,' and Stephen and I were left on
our own together, which didn't happen that often, what with the
shifts we both worked.

'Your dad hadn't noticed we took that picture,' I said.

'What picture?'

You know, the fishy smirkers, I thought at him, and saw that
we were missing something, something hardly definable: wasn't

this our home, Geoffrey an outsider, a guest? Shouldn't there now be, between Stephen and me, some faint enjoyable hint of the conspiratorial? But there was none, and I noticed it was missing. Noticing things like that, realizing what subtleties have departed, happens only when a marriage is all but dead already, it takes a lot of vanished subtleties to make you notice the absence of one more. But I didn't want to realize this then, so I didn't.

'What picture?'

'Your mother's. The men in the boat.'

'Oh that. Oh well. He didn't care for her paintings much anyway.'

'Didn't he? Didn't he? Why not?'

Stephen shrugged.

'You won't talk to me!' I cried desperately.

'Oh, not that again . . .' He went off to bed. He was in the bathroom ages, I kept hearing him run more hot water into the bath.

I went and called Beryl.

'In-laws are the pits,' said Beryl.

'How d'you know?'

'I had 'em. Now I don't. I'm an ex-daughter-in-law. That's how.'

'Oh. God. Sorry.'

'You're a jerk,' said Beryl amiably. 'Call me if it gets rough, okay?'

'I will, I will.'

'See you.' She rang off. I was trembling. Wow, I thought. Ex-daughter-in-law. Ex-husband, ex-wife. I went and looked at myself in the kitchen mirror.

'What shall I do, oh, what shall I do?' How could I know what was right? I couldn't tell my lungs from my liver, I couldn't tell yearning from jealousy, love from pride, and at any minute my body might decide to throw out something useful for the good of the whole.

And if it knew what the good of the whole was, why couldn't it, why didn't it, why wasn't it telling me?

That holiday, that fortnight, we did all the things we'd planned: took Geoffrey to the mountains, went on a sleigh-ride, hired him skis, visited the thermal springs. Geoffrey talked about health-care, about his yoghurt machine, his juice-extractor

('I'm a fruit-juice man these days'), about what all that sugar was doing to my teeth, did I not realize? and how his doctor had told him he had the blood pressure of a man of thirty.

'You'll be needing that,' said Stephen. That was the only direct attack he made. We were sitting in the thermal springs at the time, all in our bathing costumes while the snow gently fell. The water steamed, the light snow fell.

'You'll be needing that.' Just the one sneer. That was all. Otherwise he was polite, as friendly and polite as he had been to his sister Julia, what seemed like a decade or so before, in hospital, when sickness had made him look like me.

'You'll be needing that.'

Geoffrey was getting married: he'd met someone on his holiday in October, a continental cruise. She was a doctor, in the same field, as it happened, as Stephen.

'She'd be your boss, lad!' Geoffrey had said, jocularly, before he'd quite understood how the basic information was going over.

'It's rather . . . Oedipal?' I'd said that first evening he'd told us, when Geoffrey had gone off to bed in a bit of a huff.

'*Is* it.' Stephen couldn't keep still, he walked to and fro in front of the windows. He cracked his knuckles. '*Is* it.'

'I'm sorry, I wasn't joking, I was trying to –'

'Trying to what, trying to what! You think you can talk this over, you can always talk, you can talk yourself into anything, well I can't, I can't, but I know what I'm doing, I don't have to talk talk talk about it –'

'Stephen –'

'I was sorry for him, I was going to look after him! I was going to get him to stay here with us, well, that's out, that's out, he can look after himself from now on, the bastard!'

Such hatred, such real drama; I was thrilled as well as horrified, my hands pressed to my mouth.

'You think he's a nice old boy, eh?' said Stephen jeeringly. 'So happy for him, right? Bastard. He made her life a fucking misery, he was always screwing around, he never let up –'

'Oh no –'

'Oh yes, and you know what? She won a scholarship when she was young, to the Slade. The Slade! And she didn't go, she gave it up, she married him instead, the bastard!'

I saw her face poised over the sauceboat, Thank you, that's very kind of you, but do you know, I prefer to do the silver myself. And Geoffrey hidden beneath his hat told stories to his fishing mates, the latest conquest, the latest deception.

'Why didn't she just, I mean, why didn't she – '

'Leave him? Live in some flat on the dole? She had nothing, there wasn't anything she could do . . .'

Oh yes there was, I thought, there were small items of revenge, Barth not bath, darling, and the stately glittering houseful of finely polished venom.

'Stephen – '

'I'm going out.'

'Oh where, please, don't – '

'Leave me alone!'

The door slammed behind him. I'd gone to bed when he got back. It was dawn. I'd stopped crying.

'Hallo.' He sat down on the bed. He was very white, his face looked almost bluish in the half-light.

'I'm sorry.'

I sat up and put my arms round him, and rocked him back and forth.

'I'm so sorry.'

'It's all right, it's all right.'

'I do love you.'

I went on holding him. But I was thinking, quite sharply: Oh, you do, do you? Well that's as maybe, but do I love you?

So it may have looked like a reconciliation. But it felt like something else.

It was a relief to get back to work, in a way. I felt very tired all the time though, sometimes I hardly had the energy to do what was needed. I didn't get nearly so many thank-you cards. I even called Dr Phelan on time. And I kept feeling frightened, a sort of generalized fear, for my patients, their babies, myself. Understand: it was a centre of excellence, Tabor General. Ginette Derby had been no great exception. Complexities of what was in simplicity a botched job already came roaring in from all over the province: massive ante-partum haemorrhages, baroque uterine deformities, fulminating eclampsia, inter-uterine deaths. There seemed no end to the things women's bodies could do to their owners; lose you not just a toe or two, but your eldest daughter, your health for good, your life itself.

And yet, and yet ... sitting now preoccupied anywhere, at home or in the car while Stephen drove, a hallucinatory child arrived from nowhere, sat nestled in my lap for me to put my arms round; a completely involuntary piece of imagining, that I'd have squirmily disapproved of if I'd read about it in some women's magazine. I saw the reality every day; it was my body that stayed sentimental.

At work I'd attend some loving couple in chaos, and remember that Stephen would never watch so with me, hiding his face in my shoulder, he'd never laugh like that, for joy, over his new son. I kept noticing my own forearms, spying out the veins, that's a good one, I could get a Quik-cath in that one ... Increasingly now I swopped places in my mind, me for her, nurse for patient, that man for mine.

No wonder I was getting fewer thank-you cards. Bitterness, envy, fear, longing. Sum total: paralysis.

May, already. The snow turned slushy and black at the edges. In England now, tulips would be taking over from the daffodils.

Beryl Best was leaving.

'We may be earning four times what you'd get back home in dear old England,' said Beryl, 'but it still ain't enough.' She was going into real estate.

'I'll be real good at it too. Nurses are good at telling lies.'

We went out for a farewell drink, Beryl and I and several other unit 47 nurses. Beryl and I were the only ones who didn't have children. We talked about work, of course, babies, always babies, in general, the world's. I got drunk. I'd been getting drunk rather easily ever since my liver had taken such a hammering the year before. One cocktail and me and my liver were practically under the table.   ·

I drank two cocktails, and I talked too much.

'Cheat on him,' said Lynne Forester.

'Makes sense,' said Beryl.

'That's what the unit clerk did, you know Sue Finch, the unit clerk on 45? She was my patient last year, she made holes in her diaphragm, she told me when her old man had gone out to tele- phone, you know, the fourth stage of labour, calling your in-laws? He's off and she says, Look at him happy as a clam and all down to me and my darning needle!'

We laughed drunkenly and Lynne said again, 'Yup, me and my darning needle,' and we went on laughing, until I began to cry, and had to be taken to the ladies, where I wasn't sick, though I felt it.

'What shall I do, Beryl? Tell me what to do.'

'Perhaps you should go home for a while.'

'It'd finish us.'

'Yes?'

'He's my family, I can't divorce my family.'

'No, I guess not,' said Beryl.

Of course I'd already thought of cheating. But I'd told myself I wasn't quite that desperate yet. The trouble was that I was perfectly desperate enough, and knew it; it was fear that held me back. I doubted his love, and I doubted mine. Besides, I'd looked after Ginette Derby.

I'd thought at the time that, should her sort of disaster ever be my turn, I'd be able to share out the event as she had, that I'd have the sorrow, my attendant the horror. But lately it seemed to me that this would not happen, that I had too much inside knowledge, I'd seen too much reality. I would guess the truth no matter what they told me. And if I cheated on Stephen, dragged him into such a scene without his consent, where could I look to for comfort? I'd be on my own, with the horror.

'I just don't know what to do,' I told Beryl, drying my eyes on a paper towel. 'I just don't know what to do.'

But the next day I looked after someone called Twyla Deering, and made up my mind after all. Twyla Deering. I don't suppose Twyla remembers me at all. I remember her though. Name, face, date of birth: the whole lot. Twyla Deering: I remember her all right.

She arrived almost ready to deliver, hanging half out of the wheelchair her distraught mother was running along with, both of them gasping and crying with panic and relief at having made it to the hospital with the baby still inside.

Of course it's best to have a face you know beside you when you're in labour, your husband if you've got one, a friend if you haven't. But I can't approve of mothers. I draw the line there. It just seems too much to ask, to me. What could be worse than to sit beside your own daughter, watching her chaos, remembering your own, feeling both? And often my patients called for their mothers, grown women on baby two or three, groaning Oh Mum, oh Mommy – not wanting their present mothers, you understand, but the omnipotent creature of infancy. A present mother called to from chaos isn't going to see that, though; she hears the cry in the present, when all she can do is hold her daughter's hand, and suffer along with her: it's too much to ask.

Twyla Deering's mother thought so too, it seemed. She was ready to go as soon as Twyla was safely in bed, she sobbed in the doorway and blew her nose on a mangled bit of Kleenex all black with wet mascara. She didn't look like someone's mother, she had tight white trousers on and dyed golden hair.

'I gotta go now,' said Twyla's mother, going. If I'd had time I might have wondered at this show of what appeared to be grief, but I was too busy. Too appalled.

'So you're, what, seventeen?'

'Yeah –'

'Who's your doctor?'

'I don't have one.'

'You haven't seen a doctor at all?'

'Not since I found out, oh God –'

Pause. ('Deep breaths now, that's it, very good.')

'When are you due?'

'I don't know.'

'When was your last period then? Roughly?'

'Oh, I don't know, oh God, oh –'

All the time I'm asking this I'm busy. I've already got two other nurses getting my delivery room ready for me just in case, people don't hang out of wheelchairs like that for nothing. But I can't work out how the baby's lying, I paddle about with my hands, hopefully, like the DMO feeling for a liver edge; and why is the uterus so small, barely above the umbilicus? And I can't find the foetal heart. Not with my stethoscope. Not with the Sonicaid. Not with the monitor. Nothing. Checked below all I can feel is a cervical rim and bulging membranes.

'When did the pains start?'

'I don't know, about six . . .'

I press the emergency bell. My hands are shaking. My hangover's gone: just like that.

'Call paeds, will you. I need a Resident and a hand here, please – '

Running the bed down to the delivery room I'm arguing with myself the whole way. The baby's premature and dead. If I don't tell Twyla now, something like Ginette Derby's baby might slither out, in full view, unexpected. Twyla won't be able to bear such horror. Neither will I.

'Twyla, listen, listen.' I make her look at my eyes, though even then I'm not sure if she can hear me.

'Twyla, I can't hear the baby's heartbeat, I'm sorry, but I think he may be dead, I could be wrong, but I think he may be dead.'

She nods. Nothing surprises her now, how could it?

The room's full of masked strangers, two paediatricians, another nurse rummaging through the piles of paperwork for me, a startled junior Resident trembling in his rubber gloves.

'Okay now Twyla, the doctor's going to break the membranes and the baby's going to be born, okay, you're doing beautifully now Twyla, that's very good, slow breaths, that's very good – '

A gush of liquor, thick with meconium; the usual tinned-carrots smell. Twyla pushes; the baby's little white wet bottom swings rather gaily out and up from below the pubic arch, those outer doors of cushioned bone. I'm holding my breath: another dead breech, another one –

The Resident swings the child's dangling body up; moving on automatic I suction the baby's nose and mouth as the head clears the perineal floor. And the lips twitch, the nose snuffles, and the baby bawls as the paeds close in.

'Wow,' says Twyla, lying back.

'You may say Wow,' says the Resident, mock-solemn and repressing titters of relief, I can tell from his voice. 'You may say that.'

Well, everyone cleared off quite quickly after that, except the Resident, who was sewing up. Twyla seemed to be asleep, she didn't say much, except that she could use a cigarette. I went to put some dry wraps on the baby. He was tiny. Not premature, but undergrown, the sort of baby you tend to get if you eat badly and go on smoking and knocking back gins: long for his weight, skinny, with a thin simian old-man's face. He sucked fiercely at his little skinny hands, he looked anxious, his small monkey-face simply worried. Small-for-dates babies are all like that, born anxious, worried about where the next meal's coming from.

I turned round to Twyla: 'God, I'm really sorry I scared you like that.'

'That's okay.'

'You want to hold him now?' A formality, asking that; but she said, 'No – I don't wanna see him. I'm' (she lowered her voice, she didn't want the doctor to hear) 'I'm having him adopted.'

For a moment all my feelings were centred on myself, aghast at having made two such awful blunders in so short a time, and with the same woman.

'Oh no, I'm so sorry, I should have found out earlier, oh Lord.'

'That's okay,' said Twyla, sounding as if it really was, as if she'd shrug her shoulders if she weren't lying down. I remembered her mother's anguish, the blackened tatter of Kleenex held to her swollen crying eyes.

'Right, well then,' I say, 'I'll tell you what I'm going to do, I'm going to get you all cleaned up, or would you rather get up for a shower? Then you can get some sleep.'

'Can I smoke?'

'Sure, there's a dayroom –' I'm very friendly, I'm extra-careful friendly, I'll be non-judgemental if it kills me. I shoot off to the desk to change the post-partum bed for a gynae one, call the nursery, fire an imaginary pistol at my head to Lynne Forester, who's writing up a case in the record book ('She's adopting, I didn't know, I asked her if she wanted to hold the baby!' 'Oh no, you did?'), dash back with a glass of milk for Twyla, who'd admitted, pressed, that she could drink this.

'Right, I'm just going to take the baby round now –'

'Oh. Can I see him?'

'Of course.'

I park the plastic crib beside her. She looks. She's still hanging on to her glass, there's a faint rim of milk on her upper lip.

'Okay, thanks.'

Is there anything I should say? Should I risk anything else?

'If you should er, change your mind –'

'Sure. It's okay. Okay?'

'Right.'

There was no one in the nursery when I got there. No one adult, I mean, just a few babies asleep. I sat down in one of the low nursing chairs and picked Twyla's baby up. He was asleep,

I jiggled him until he woke up. It was a long time since I'd held a baby, I'd stopped wanting to hold other women's babies long ago. But now I held Twyla's skinny little baby in the crook of my arm, against my heart. You'll be all right now, I thought at him. She's having you adopted.

I didn't think about Twyla, about how awful it must be for her to give up her baby, how much she would eventually regret doing so, how she'd remember his birthdays and wonder how tall he was this year, and whether he looked like her, and did he have a girlfriend yet, and was she a grandmother by now? I didn't consider Twyla, not then. I was on the baby's side.

One of the baby's skinny arms moved, worked free of the blanket. I caught the miniature fingers in my mouth, and held them for a moment, very gently, between my lips. I was on the baby's side. Common, perhaps, to childless midwives: by virtue of the work I'd somehow joined the club of motherhood, which always puts the baby first, which says, If you're a baby's mother, that's primarily what you are. I had come to feel this, but without the proper focus.

'Tell you something,' I said to the baby, 'I think I'm in the wrong job.' This made me giggle; for a moment I rocked the baby and laughed to myself. I felt quite peaceful, it was so quiet in the nursery, and the baby felt very nice. I thought about how awful my job was. I decided that if my marriage had been happier, I'd have given up the job long ago; then I realized that if the job had been happier, I'd have given up on my marriage faster too. Seeing this also made me smile. More than a year of horrors! It had felt like faithful endurance; had it perhaps been just fear all along?

'It looks that way,' I told the baby, 'and look what happened to his mother. Yes. Whose fault was that? Hmm?' Perfect fear, that holds all the doors closed against you.

I thought of Stephen's silence, his furious inarticulacy, and saw that it was not merely a handicap, to be pitied, as I had thought, but armour, and a weapon in his hands.

'And what's he offering me? Sod all, that's what. Sod all. It's me going crazy, not him. So why am I putting up with it? After all, he's not really family. He's not family after all. He's not my flesh-and-blood. Now if I were to take you home with me, you'd be my flesh-and-blood. An adult and a baby: that's family. See?

The baby looked back. I held him at just the right distance, so that he could focus on my face.

'See?'

The nursery nurse came in.

'Oh, hi, is that the – '

'Yes.'

'You do a blood sugar?'

'Low but not too low.'

'You look real cosy, you want to feed him?'

'No, I've got to get back, thanks.' I stood up and handed the baby over. 'Goodbye now.' I can still see his face, his little aged-monkey face. Goodbye now: goodbye.

Then I went back to Twyla and carried on being friendly.

The apartment was empty when I got back that evening. Stephen must have been and gone, the place was a bit steamy, and there was a faint smell of some new aftershave on the air. As I packed my suitcase it struck me for the first time, really for the first time, that he might be seeing someone else, all those long baths and extra shaves, weren't they classic signs?

Well, I mustn't think about that, not if it hurts, I said to myself. I called the airport. I could get a standby ticket to Miami that very night; be home the following day. I called my mother, and was surprised by the degree of her sympathy, as if I'd expected her to be angry.

'I'll come and meet you any time,' she shouted, no fussing about what time it was or how far apart we were, not that time.

'Wonderful, wonderful,' I shouted back. I don't know why we were shouting.

Then I called a few friends to say goodbye. Beryl was out. I told myself I'd write. Then I wrote to unit 47's head nurse, not the fierce polemic I'd more than once imagined but a polite farewell, plus an apology for not giving any notice.

Then Stephen. No point in indulging in any explanations. He favoured the terse, didn't he? Despised volubility?

I tore a sheet of paper from the notepad, and wrote on it in capitals:

GOODBYE

and then allowed myself a touch of theatricality: I tucked the note behind his mother's picture, the fishy smirkers.

I put the door key on the table.

I remembered my well-loved Chevrolet, and thought a goodbye at it.

I went and looked for the last time at the night-time Hollywood city. As ever, it spoke to me, it sang me a very faint chorus:

> Come on along and listen to (rat tat-a-tat)
> The lullaby of Broadway . . .

'Some other time,' I thought to myself, and I gently closed the door behind me.

Printed in the United Kingdom
by Lightning Source UK Ltd.
122771UK00001B/100/A